DOLLAR BILL

DOLLAR BILL

SHAWN SMITH

iUniverse LLC
Bloomington

DOLLAR BILL

iUniverse books may be ordered through booksellers or by contacting:

iUniverse LLC
1663 Liberty Drive
Bloomington, IN 47403
www.iuniverse.com
1-800-Authors (1-800-288-4677)

ISBN: 978-1-4917-3181-9 (sc)
ISBN: 978-1-4917-3182-6 (e)

Printed in the United States of America.

iUniverse rev. date: 04/16/2014

It is the summer of 1997. On a sunny and bright Friday afternoon on Long Beach Blvd. in Compton. DOLLAR BILL, the only white boy on the street, is walking his bike with one flat tire into a gas station. He is 11 years old, slim and tall for his age. A guy (CROW) and a GIRL pull up in a brand new Ford Expedition truck with 22" tires and chrome wheels and park by a gas pump

CROW

You want something inside, baby?

GIRL

Yeah, get me a soda. Hey, who love you baby?

CROW

I know you do.

Crow exits the truck and walks over to Dollar Bill who is putting air in his tire and gives him dapps.

CROW

What's up lil' homey, gimme some.

DOLLAR BILL

What's up Crow. Loan me some money, man, you rich.

CROW

> Look lil' nigga, you gotta pump the gas first, then I'll give you some paper.

Dollar Bill finishes putting air in his tire and walks over by the truck with his bike. Crow walks into the gas station. The girl is talking on her cell phone.

GIRL

> (whispering)
> Ok, he's inside paying for gas now, so hurry up.

She quickly hangs up the phone. Crow walks out of the station with the soda in his hand and returns to the truck. Dollar Bill begins pumping the gas. Crow hands him money.

CROW

> Here's five dollars lil' cuzz and you better not spill no gas.

DOLLAR BILL

> Fuck you Crow. And thanks for the five. dollars big homey.

Crow gets back into the truck, handing the soda to the girl.

CROW

> I grabbed that one from the back, nice and cold.

GIRL

> Crow, you so sweet.

CROW

> That's just my Compton charm.

A 1982 Oldsmobile Cutlass creeps into the gas station up to the drivers side window of Crow's truck and stops, with the motor still running. Inside the car are two Mexican thugs. One jumps out of the passenger side with a shotgun and shoots Crow dead on in the face. His head is blown completely off, blood and tissue splattering everywhere. The girl begins screaming hysterically as the thug jumps back into the car which peals off, tires screeching. All around people are running and screaming Dollar Bill freezes and drops the gas nozzle on the ground

Three weeks later. Inside a run down house, in a small bedroom, Dollar Bill, in boxers, wakes up, jumps out of a bunk bed, walks into the bathroom, where he pees and brushes his teeth. He walks back into the bedroom, throwing on his clothes, then walks through the living room, heading toward the front door. His MOM enters the living room from the kitchen and glares at him.

MOM

Where do you think you are going this early in the morning Dollar?

DOLLAR BILL

I'm goin up the street to play, can I?

MOM

Yea, go ahead. But you better be home before those street lights come on. You got a five minute grace period.

DOLLAR BILL

Fo sho.

Dollar Bill walks out the door and up the streets of his neighborhood in Compton to another house where a guy (CEE) is hanging out. Dollar Bill walks up to him and gives him dapps.

DOLLAR BILL

What's up Cee.

CEE

What's up lil' homey You up early.

DOLLAR BILL

Man I need some loot, Cee. Loan me some money or let me make some.

CEE

Get the fuck outa here, white boy. How the fuck you gonna make some money, you too young.

DOLLAR BILL

Gim'me a dope sack, Let me make some then.

CEE

I'll tell you what lil' homey, you wanna make some paper?

DOLLAR BILL

Doin' what?

CEE

All you gotta do is sit on the fire hydrant across the street and look out for the police. Every time you see the po-po you holla at us and let us know. Can you do that?

DOLLAR BILL

I can do that. But how do I make money by doin' that bullshit?

CEE

At the end of the day when you gotta go home, I'll give you twenty dollars. Is that cool?

DOLLAR BILL

Twenty dollars just to sit on the fire hydrant all day? Do I get a break?

CEE

Every hour you can take a ten minute break.

DOLLAR BILL

When can I start?

CEE

Right now if you want.

DOLLAR BILL

Can a nigga get half his money now in case the ice cream truck come by?

CEE

You ain't no nigga fool. You a white boy. You better watch who you say that shit to, Dollar, before somebody shoot your little white-black ass.

DOLLAR BILL

Man I grew up here, ain't nobody gonna fuck with me. I got back up for that ass. if they try.

CEE

What back up you got? Your lil' white dick as a pistol.

DOLLAR BILL

Don't be hatin' cause my dick bigger than yours, fool.

CEE

Watch your mouth boy.

DOLLAR BILL

Watch my mouth? I'm a lookout man for a drug dealer and I gotta watch my mouth. Fuck you Cee.

CEE

Here's two dollars, now get your ass on the fire hydrant.

Dollar Bill walks across the street and sits on the fire hydrant. Minutes later a beat up station wagon drives up and stops beside Dollar Bill. The driver (CRACKHEAD) says to Dollar Bill

CRACKHEAD

You got somethin'?

DOLLAR BILL

What you need?

CRACK HEAD

I need a dove.

DOLLAR BILL

Hold on for a minute.

Dollar Bill runs across the street, knocking on Cee's door. Another guy (E) answers the door.

DOLLAR BILL

Where's Cee.

E

He in the shower, what you want Dollar?

DOLLAR BILL

There's a twenty dollar sale out here waitin'!

E

Hold on

E closes the door for a moment then opens it, handing Dollar a little piece of dope in rock form.

E

Give him this. Is he walkin' or drivin'?

DOLLAR BILL

He drivin'

E

Make sure he turns the car off first and have him show you the money, so he can't snatch the dope and drive off.

Dollar Bill runs back across the street to the drivers side window of the crackhead's car.

DOLLAR BILL

Yo man. Cut the car off first. You got my money?

Crackhead turns off the ignition.

CRACK HEAD

Let me see what you workin' with first.

DOLLAR BILL

That bomb shit. See.

Dollar Bill puts his hand through the window showing him the dope. The crackhead exchanges money for the dope.

DOLLAR BILL

>Cool. When you come back next time ask for me, Dollar Bill. I got that.

Crack head pulls off. Dollar bill sits back on the fire hydrant, looking down the street. Home girls and home boys, are drinking and talking, their 64 Chevy low rider cars hoppin'. A sexy girl (CRACKHEAD 2) walks up and asks Dollar Bill

CRACKHEAD 2

>I need a dime piece.

DOLLAR BILL

>Bitch, we don't sell no mother fuckin' dime pieces, just twenties.

CRACKHEAD 2

>Don't start that shit with me Dollar, you little bastard. Where's Cee?

Cee comes walking out the door wearing only a towel and slippers carrying a small baggie in his hand.

CRACKHEAD 2

>There he is.

Crackhead walks determinedly across the street up to Cee.

CRACKHEAD 2

>Cee, can I get a dime piece, you know I'm good for it.

CEE

>Yea that's cool. Here.

Cee reaches into the baggie pulling out a tiny rock and hands it to her and she hands him a ten dollar bill. Crackhead 2, yelling, so Dollar Bill can hear.

CRACKHEAD 2

Thanks, Cee. Somebody needs to teach that little fucker Dollar some manners. I'll take my money some where else where I can buy me a dime piece and a five piece if I want.

DOLLAR BILL

Fuck you base head ass bitch I'll fuck you up.

Crack head 2 sneers at Dollar Bill and gives him the middle finger, mumbling.

CRACKHEAD 2

Wanna be nigga.

DOLLAR BILL

Bitch. What you say?

CEE

Hold on Dollar. Chill Bro.(to Crack head) Don't worry. I'll handle it, your money is always good here. (to Dollar Bill) Dollar, come here man.

Dollar Bill walks obediently across the street to Cee.

DOLLAR BILL

What's up Cee? Here's your twenty dollars from the first sale.

He hands Cee the money.

CEE

You can't be rude to the customers. That's where your money comes from. This is a business Dollar. The crack heads got you this job. Think about it . . . without base heads you wouldn't have a job. I wouldn't need you to look out for the police. See how that works? It's that simple.

DOLLAR BILL

I guess so.

A few weeks have passed. Dollar Bill is sitting on the fire hydrant. The street lights come on and Dollar Bill starts walking towards his house. He walks through the door of his house, his mom is standing in the hallway waiting with her arms crossed.

MOM

Bring your butt here Dollar.

DOLLAR BILL

What'd I do?

MOM

Where did you get all this money from I found in your room?

DOLLAR BILL

I got it from Cee and his pops. They pay me every week to clean up the yard. I ain't lyin'.

MOM

You must be guilty of something. I didn't say you was lyin' yet.

DOLLAR BILL

Mom, if you want we can go over there right now and you can ask for yourself.

MOM

I'm not gonna ask nobody nothing.

DOLLAR BILL

Well I'm just tryin' to prove my case.

MOM

Loan your mom forty dollars.

DOLLAR BILL

That's cool. Take it.

Next morning Dollar Bill is hanging out with two of his little home boys (MIKE & CRAZY), next to the fire hydrant.

MIKE

(to Dollar Bill)
I hear you rollin' now nigga.

DOLLAR BILL

A lil' somethin', somethin. You'all fools ready to lose you'alls money.

CRAZY

What you wanna play? Pitch or shoot dice?

MIKE

Let's pitch. I got a pocket full of quarters.

DOLLAR BILL

Well bring it on then, shit.

Dollar Bill, Mike and Crazy position themselves facing the curb and begin pitching quarters to the curb.

MIKE

>Here come that fool Ben with a cheeseburger and a soda in his hand. I'm about to get his ass.

DOLLAR BILL

>I'm gonna get his ass fuck that.

MIKE

>Hell no! He got my ass yesterday and slapped my ice cream outa my hand.

Another little home boy (BEN) walks up to the group and starts talking.

BEN

>What's up fools.

Mike slaps the cheeseburger out of Ben's hand and Dollar Bill slaps the soda from the other hand.

DOLLAR BILL & MIKE

>Don't Eat That!!

Dollar Bill, Mike and Crazy double over laughing hysterically.

BEN

>That's fucked up. I just bought this mother fucker. I forgot we was playin' this stupid game all week.

Cee pulls up in a Mercedes Benz and calls out.

CEE

>Dollar Bill, come here lil' homey. Peep this shit out.

Dollar Bill walks up to the window of the car. His friends follow behind him.

CEE

You want a job?

DOLLAR BILL

You already gave me a job.

CEE

You bein' promoted. Check this out. Take this dope sack and every hundred dollars worth of dope you sell, you keep twenty dollars for yourself.

Cee passes the dope sack to Dollar Bill.

DOLLAR BILL

Hell yea! That's where the real money at!

CEE

So can you handle that Dollar without fuckin' it up?

DOLLAR BILL

Man I'm about to take over this mother fucker.

CEE

Remember little homey. The crack heads are your best friends.

BEN

Cee, when you gonna hook me up with a job?

MIKE & CRAZY

Me too, me too Cee!

CEE

> I do need a new look out man since Dollar got promoted.

MIKE

> And sit outside on the fire hydrant all day? Fuck that!

CRAZY

> Hell no! It's to hot for that shit. Gimme another job Cee.

CEE

> That's the shit I'm talkin' about. You lil' niggas wanna be rich but don't wanna pay your dues. Fuck you lil' niggas man.

Cee pulls off, makes a u-turn and drives off in the opposite direction.

DOLLAR BILL

> Don't hate lil' homeys. When I get rich I'll give you all a job.

BEN

> Hey Dollar, I'll sit on the fire hydrant for you.

DOLLAR BILL

> Well get on it then. I'll give you ten bucks a day.

Two years later. Dollar Bill, is driving up his street in a brand new canary yellow convertible 5.0 Mustang with 20" chromed rims. His music is playing loudly, as he passes by his home boys, they all motion "what's up" with their hands in the air. All the girls wave and holler for his attention.

GIRLS

> Dollar, call me later, my mom be at work!

Dollar Bill smiles and nods at everyone in acknowledgement.

Later that night Dollar is lying on his bed in his room. He is startled by a loud crash. Several police kick down his door and surround him, shouting and pointing their guns in his face.

POLICE 1

> Get on the fucking floor! Now! Put your hands behind your back! Do it now!

Dollar Bill methodically follows their directions. The police handcuff him and pull him to his feet. Other officers are ram-sacking the house.

DOLLAR BILL

> What the fuck you doing fool. Get your mother fuckin' hands off me! You got a mother fuckin search warrant?

POLICE 1

> Right here in my hand. You're under arrest for possession and sales of a controlled substance.

DOLLAR BILL

> Damn!

Five years later. Dollar Bill, now 6'2" tall, handsome with an athletic build, is walking out of the prison gates. Two armed guards follow him and unlock the gate. Dollar Bill walks out alone. His mom and brother are waiting outside by their car. Dollar Bill smiling walks over to his family embracing them. They get in the car and drive off without looking back.

The sun is setting as the car pulls into the driveway of the modest duplex. They all get out of the car, mom leading the way into the house.

MOM

> Dollar, how do you like the new place? We probably moved at least three times in the last five years.

DOLLAR BILL

> Mom, anything is better than be locked up behind bars like an animal.

Inside is a stack of boxes taped up with Dollar Bill's name on them. He begins unpacking personal items, designer clothes, animal skinned boots, shoes, belts, etc, some with the tags still on them. Mom and his BROTHER sit on the couch happily watching Dollar Bill.

BROTHER

> Was that one guard Bill Starrs still working there? I hated that fool?

DOLLAR BILL

> That fool still workin' there. Matter of fact, I was in the same unit you was in.

BROTHER

> That fool love him some John Wayne. He'd fuck you up for saying fuck the duke.

DOLLAR BILL

> No shit. Bill got this one white boy for saying fuck John Wayne, man he picked the fool up off his feet and slammed his ass on the ground hard! Hey, what ever happened to that bitch who got the home boy Crow smoked?

BROTHER

> That ho just disappeared.

DOLLAR BILL

> You know how many real niggas in the pen right now over a bitch?! And how many O.G.'s we lost over bitches? That's why I always tell a motha fucka "never trust a bitch"!!

Next morning Dollar Bill, in boxers, gets out of bed and walks to the bathroom where he pees and brushes his teeth. He returns to the bedroom and dresses. He grabs a bike which is leaning against the wall and walks out to the living room. Mom is sitting at the table working a puzzle.

MOM

> Where do you think are going this early in the morning Dollar?

DOLLAR BILL

> I'm about to roll over Grams house. I'll be back later.

MOM

> You be careful now. I love you.

DOLLAR BILL

> I'll be alright mom. The hood is just right next door. Peace out. I love you to.

Dollar Bill is riding the bike down the street in the neighborhood. He stops in front of another modest house. Outside he sees two homeboys (COUSIN TRA & Mike) hanging out. Dollar Bill gives his homeboys dapps.

COUSIN TRA

> Dollar, what's up cousin. Your brother said you was out nigga. I know you got some money put up.

MIKE

> What's up Dollar. I ain't seen your ass in years, since they raided your pad, nigga. How long you been down?

DOLLAR BILL

> Five years. I would've been out sooner on good behavior but me and some of the homeys' fucked these fools up for tryin' to cheat us in a dice game.

A home boy (BONE) in a Cherokee Jeep, music bumping, pulls over and jumps out to embrace Dollar Bill.

BONE

> I didn't think your ass was ever comin' home. When I got paroled I heard you was up there locin' up.

In the background, Cousin Tra pulls a roll of bills from his pocket, counting it, and then putting it away.

DOLLAR BILL

> My nig! What's up Dog. What you been up to?

BONE

> I m up there in San Bernadino gettin' my ends, nigga.

DOLLAR BILL

> I feel you.

BONE

> I tried to get a regular job but cause I been in prison no body won't hire me. I tried over and over and over to do this shit legal, no luck. So I'm back on the street again selling dope and taggin' cars.

DOLLAR BILL

Once you go to prison and do your time you always gonna be a criminal in societies eyes. You can never pay your debt to society. When I was locked up I seen niggas' get out and come right back.

BONE

And you know why? Because they couldn't get a job. Nobody would hire 'em with a prison record. But they got families to feed so they turn back to crime to survive.

MIKE

The government will pay forty thousand dollars a year to lock up one inmate but they won't pay us thirty thousand a year to make an honest living. So where do we go from there?

COUSIN TRA

Back to prison.

BONE

Man I don't wanna talk about this shit no more. I might snap.

DOLLAR BILL

So what's up with San Bernadino, Bone?

BONE

Man I got that shit sewed up. I'm headed back tonight, you wanna roll?

DOLLAR BILL

Hell yea, I'm rollin'. I might as well start makin' my money now, fuck that.

BONE

> I'm about to shake this spot. Peace out.
> Bone gets back in the jeep and drives off.

DOLLAR BILL

> Tra, lend me five dollars nigga.

COUSIN TRA

> I ain't got it' dog.

DOLLAR BILL

> Cuzz, you just stood right there and counted out at least three hundred dollars in front of me.

COUSIN TRA

> I can't do shit dog. I need all of mine. I'm short.

DOLLAR BILL

> That's fucked up. Before I went to jail I took care of your ass. gave your ass money, bought your ass clothes, and now I can't even borrow five bucks! Fuck you nigga, that's cool.

Later that night. Dollar Bill and Bone pull up in the Cherokee Jeep at an apartment building and get out. Dollar Bill grabs a bag from the back seat and follows Bone through the gate, up the stairs, to an apartment. Bone unlocks the door and they walk inside.

DOLLAR BILL

> I like this place. Whose pad is this?

BONE

> I live alone nigga. I ain't gonna have no bitch dippin' in and out of my shit. The landlord's a crack head, so there ain't no credit check. Just give the bitch some dope and she be happy.

DOLLAR BILL

   Unbelievable.

Dollar Bill walks to the window and looks out. Outside he sees a sexy, caramel-skinned, black girl (SUNNY) with delicate features and long silky hair, talking to another girl

DOLLAR BILL

   Bone, come here dog!

Bone joins Dollar Bill at the window.

BONE

   What's up?

DOLLAR BILL

   Who's that bitch right there? The one with the big ass in the tight dress?

BONE

   Oh Sunny? That stuck up bitch ain't fuckin' with no body. Fuck that bitch. You wastin' your time. There's a lot of hood rats around here you can holla at.

DOLLAR BILL

   Fuck what you talkin' about I'm about. to get that bitch.

Dollar bill walks away from the window, back outside and down the stairs headed towards Sunny.

DOLLAR BILL

   Yo.

Sunny stopping and turning around as Dollar walks up to her.

DOLLAR BILL

What's up. I'm Dollar bill. How you doin'?

SUNNY

How you doin' Dollar bill? I'm Sunny.

DOLLAR BILL

Not good enough. I don't have you yet.

SUNNY

You're kinda cute for a white boy. Why they call you Dollar Bill?

DOLLAR BILL

When I was a kid I was always tryin' to make a dollar outa fifteen cent. So the name kinda stuck to me.

SUNNY

Interesting story. I never seen you around here before. You just moved in?

DOLLAR BILL

No, I'm here with my dog Bone.

SUNNY

That pervert. He always tryin' to get some ass. He know he ain't getting' shit here.

DOLLAR BILL

Well not to be rude or disrespectful, but you have a nice big ass. Can I touch it?

SUNNY

I ain't never had a man ask me could he touch my ass before. I know you ain't from around here. Where you from?

DOLLAR BILL

  I'm from Compton.

SUNNY

  Oh you from the hood. You cool. You can touch.

Dollar bill reaches over and squeezes the ass

DOLLAR BILL

  Damn! I haven't felt an ass like that in years.

SUNNY

  You just got out of prison, huh?

DOLLAR BILL

  Damn. Is it written all over my face?

SUNNY

  Nope. But niggas from Compton ain't that nice to bitches like me.

DOLLAR BILL

  I don't think you're a bitch. I just think you're misunderstood.

SUNNY

  I like that. I got a motel room around the corner. Wanna come over later on?

DOLLAR BILL

  Hell yea.

SUNNY

  I'll pick you up at midnight.

Inside a cheap motel room. Sunny and Dollar Bill are on the bed naked. Sunny is on top riding him aggressively. As they kiss passionately. Dollar Bill then throws her over on her back grabbing her hands over her head and penetrates her again forcefully. He begins humping her like a runaway train as she screams in pleasure. He finally reaches climax and collapses next to her, drenched in sweat.

SUNNY

Did you like it?

DOLLAR BILL

Did I like it? Feel my legs girl, I'm shakin' shit.

SUNNY

I think I'm in love. Do you believe in love at first sight? Or do you believe in hit it and run.

DOLLAR BILL

I know my dick is in love right now.

SUNNY

Fuck you nigga.

DOLLAR BILL

Ha, Ha. I'm just playing, girl. Have a sense of humor. I haven't had pussy in five years, shit. What you want me to say? But to answer your question, love at first sight is a part of nature.

SUNNY

Thanks Dollar.

The phone rings three times. Sunny reaches over to the nightstand and answers the phone.

SUNNY

Hello . . . uh-huh . . . ok . . . in 15 minutes . . . I'll be
there . . . Bye.

She hangs up the phone.

SUNNY

Dollar, can you do me a favor?

DOLLAR BILL

It depends on the favor.

SUNNY

This guy owes me some money and I need you to
watch my back in case he trip.

DOLLAR BILL

I been whoopin' ass for five years. One more ain't
gonna matter. Let's roll.

Sunny and Dollar Bill drive up in a Camaro into the parking lot of
another motel.

SUNNY

I'll be in room 69 but don't let him see you, or he
might get spooked. If I'm not out in twenty minutes
come and get me.

DOLLAR BILL

Sixty-nine. I like that number. Go handle your
business.

Sunny exits the vehicle and walks up the stairs. Dollar Bill watches
her appreciatively. She enters the room and he waits patiently until she
reappears. Sunny gets back into the drivers seat and driving off, she
hands him money.

SUNNY

Here baby, take this three hundred dollars.

DOLLAR BILL

Three hundred dollars is a lot of money just for watching some bodies back. You sure you ain't robbed the mother fucker?

SUNNY

It's your money. You deserve it daddy. I choose you. You the one now.

DOLLAR BILL

What the fuck you talking about? You choose me?

SUNNY

I'm a ho.

DOLLAR BILL

Bitch you a what?

SUNNY

I'm a prostitute. I sell pussy for a livin'. That's what I do.

DOLLAR BILL

Why didn't you tell me this shit at first before you brought me over here?

SUNNY

I didn't want to scare you off.

DOLLAR BILL

Don't you ever put me in a fuckin' situation like this again when I don't know what the fuck is goin' on.

SUNNY

> I'm sorry. But listen Dollar, we both need somethin'. You need money and I need a man. I need somebody to watch my back. Somebody I can trust. who can take charge.

DOLLAR BILL

> You don't even know me like that girl. Don't play me.

SUNNY

> You want the money or not? If not give it back.

DOLLAR BILL

> Alright, alright. I'll keep it. So what do we do next?

SUNNY

> We go to Hollywood and get paid!

Next day. Dollar Bill and Sunny are driving down Sunset Blvd. In Hollywood. They pull into a cheap motel. And park.

SUNNY

> Use some of the money I gave you and get a room for three nights.

DOLLAR BILL

> I'll be right back.

Dollar bill gets out of the car and enters the motel office. Behind the desk is an Asian clerk.

DOLLAR BILL

> How you doin'? How much for one night for two people?

HOTELCLERK

>   (Heavy Asian accent)
> Fifty five dollar plus tax. Five dollar for remote
> control, ten dollar for phone and five dollar for key.
> Total is eighty-two dollar!.

DOLLAR BILL

> Give me a room for the night.

Dollar Bill throws down the money and takes the key.

HOTELCLERK

> And no visitors or you go! Don't want no problem
> here!

Entering the motel room, Dollar Bill sets the bags down and they both
relax on the bed and remove all their clothes.

SUNNY

> I'm so tired, we been up all night. How many days
> you get the room for?

DOLLAR BILL

> Three days, like you said. I'm goin' to sleep.

Night falls. Driving down Sunset Blvd. In Sunny's car, Dollar Bill pulls
over.

DOLLAR BILL

> You be careful. I'll be watchin' you.

SUNNY

> If I need anything I'll throw up my hands.

Sunny, wearing a green mini-dress and clear stripper shoes with a tiny
matching bag, gets out of the car. Dollar bill drives off.

Further down Sunset Blvd. a car is pulled over. Inside, a TRICK talks to a PROSTITUTE who is leaning on the window.

TRICK 1

Need a ride?

PROSTITUTE 1

Sure do. Where you goin'; cutie.

TRICK 1

Wherever you wanna go. Hop in.

PROSTITUTE 1

You look like a cop. Are you a cop?

TRICK 1

No, I ain't no cop. Trust me.

PROSTITUTE 1

Well show me somethin' that a cop wouldn't show me if you're not a cop.

TRICK 1

Like what?

PROSTITUTE 1

I'm cool. I don't want a ride? Bye.

TRICK 1

Wait a minute. Look.

Trick 1 unzips his pants and reveals his penis. The prostitute jumps in the car and they drive off.

PROSTITUTE 1

So what you wanna do?

TRICK 1

> I want you to suck my dick and then I wanna fuck your pretty lil' ass.

PROSTITUTE 1

> That's gonna cost you sixty dollars cutie. Money first.

The trick pulls over into an alley and parks, handing her the money.

TRICK 1

> Here's your money.

PROSTITUTE 1

> Relax cutie. Take your pants off so I can suck it and get it hard.

Trick removes his pants and the ho begins sucking his dick. Then he pulls up her dress and climbs on top of her and begins fucking her. A pimp (PIMP 1), dressed in baggy jeans, a jersey and tennis shoes, creeps up from behind the car and jerks open the passenger door.

PIMP 1

> Get the fuck out fore I shoot your mother fuckin' ass nigga.

The trick jumps up quickly, as the prostitute leaps out of the car.

TRICK 1

> Please don't shoot! Just take what you want!

PROSTITUTE 1

> (to pimp)
> Damn, it took you long enough!

PIMP 1

> Bitch, shut the fuck up and grab his pants ho!

PROSTITUTE 1

> Gimme those fuckin pants trick, and that wedding band.

The trick trembles in fear as the prostitute grabs his wallet from his pants.

TRICK 1

> Please let me keep my wedding band. I'm a married man.

PIMP 1

> Fuck you! You should'a thought about your wife instead of bein' out here buyin' pussy. You takin' too long!

The pimp puts the gun to the tricks' head and fires two times, blowing the tricks' brains out and shattering the window.

PROSTITUTE 1

> Why you shoot him?

PIMP 1

> Shut the fuck up bitch, before I shoot your ass too. Get his shit and let's go.

She grabs his wallet and takes the ring off his finger. They both run off down the alley and jump into a parked, 1989 Honda and speed off turning onto Sunset Blvd. Dollar Bill watches the car, with no head lights race by.

Dollar Bill is looking all around him as he drives down the track. There are prostitutes everywhere, all ages and colors, walking, hanging out and leaning in car windows. Dollar Bill pulls up into the parking lot of a strip club. Several pimps are hanging out by the cars. Dollar Bill, wearing a black silk shirt, black Italian slacks, and peanut butter ostrich boots with matching belt, parks and exits the vehicle He walks over to one of the pimps (TIGER), giving him dapps.

TIGER

What's up player?

DOLLAR BILL

Clockin' that money, baby.

TIGER

I haven't seen a white player since I got outa prison.

A prostitute, (PROSTITUE 2) dressed in cut off daisy dukes and high heeled boots crosses the street. She hands Tiger some money and he begins counting it.

TIGER

Bitch, don't bring your ass over here like that interrupting me when I'm talking to another player. Two hundred dollars? Bitch you better get your punk ass out there and get my money right ho. You been short the last god damned three weeks. (to Dollar) Sorry about that young player. See these hos' run around here crazy sometimes. They don't know their pussy from their mouth. (to prostitute) Bitch. Why you still here. Go get my trap money ho.

PROSTITUTE 2

There's a lot of hos' working tonight, all of Jumbo's girls are out here so it's hard to catch a date.

TIGER.

Bitch I don't give a fuck who hos' out tonight. Go do your duty and serve your country. Where my wife at?

PROSTITUTE 2

On a date.

TIGER

Are you hungry?

PROSTITUTE 2

Not yet.

TIGER

Then get the fuck out of here.

The prostitute walks back across the street joining a group of hos'.

TIGER

By the way I'm Tiger.

DOLLAR BILL

Call me Dollar Bill.

TIGER

Haven't seen you around here before young player. New to the game?

DOLLAR BILL

No T baby, I ain't new to the game. I been pimpin' in Compton. Just tryin' to step it up a little bit and get that real money.

TIGER

Well, I welcome you to the upgrade, but watch these hos' Dollar, they will try to get over on you and shit. Where your bitch at?

DOLLAR BILL

Up the street getting' my money.

TIGER

> See that black stallion I was talkin' to. That bitch been in my stable for a year now. That hos' got a college degree from Harvard.

DOLLAR BILL

> No shit. A ho with a college degree. Unbelievable.

TIGER

> Society got the game fucked up. They think every pimp and every ho on the street doesn't have any knowledge, that they all jail birds and ghetto hos'. See Dollar, one thing about this game, all pimps and hos' are different. Some got 9 to 5 jobs, some are teachers, some are lawyers. And some are full time pimps and hos'.

DOLLAR BILL

> That's some real shit. And they think every pimp wears a fur coat and drives a Cadillac.

TIGER

> Now you feel me. You know what young player? There's a lot of white pimps out here who don't get their pimpin' rights. So you put them on the map baby.

DOLLAR BILL

> Thanks T baby. I feel you pimpin'.

TIGER

> I prefer to be called a business man. I don't pimp hos'. With all due respect, these hos' choose you, you don't choose the hos. We can't make a bitch do nothin' she don't wanna do. Society thinks we keep them drugged up and hold them hostage and force

them to turn tricks. A ho sells pussy cause she want to, not cause we tell her to.

DOLLAR BILL

That shit deep. How many hos' you got T baby if you don't mind me askin'?

TIGER

Five of the baddest hos' on the track and I'm married to my bottom bitch. I love that ho so god damned much I married her.

DOLLAR BILL

Preach on, businessman, preach on. I'll peep you later T baby, I gotta go check on my bitch.

Dollar Bill gets back in the car and pulls back on Sunset Blvd. All around him other pimps are cruising slowly up and down the track, where hos' are still out in full force. Dollar Bill spots Sunny walking with another girl. He pulls over and Sunny jumps in. to the car and they drive off.

DOLLAR BILL

Bitch you got somethin' for me?

SUNNY

Here's a hundred and fifty dollars. It's slow out here. Too many bitches out here workin' I can't make shit. What you been doin'?

DOLLAR BILL

Talkin' to a pimp named Tiger.

SUNNY

He good people. He don't beat his hos'.

DOLLAR BILL

> You hungry? Let's get somethin' to eat.

SUNNY

> I thought you'd never ask.

DOLLAR BILL

> I'm gonna stop by the motel first and pay for two more days.

SUNNY

> You told me you paid for three days already. Dollar, you lied to me.

DOLLAR BILL

> I only paid for one day in case anything went wrong, like if you got arrested, I'd have money to bail you out of jail.

SUNNY

> That's make sense. But you still lied to me.

DOLLAR BILL

> Shut the fuck up and listen. You always gotta have a back up plan. That's why I'm in charge.

Inside Dennys, Dollar Bill and Sunny are sitting at a booth eating.

SUNNY

> See that pimp over there with his hos'. See the one girl staring at you and lustin'?

DOLLAR BILL

> I see that ho. I'll give that bitch five years of dickin'.

SUNNY

See what she doin'? She "wreck less eye ballin'" you. Now if we was on the track and she look at you like that, smilin' and lustin', you could break that ho.

DOLLAR BILL

I don't wanna break her, I wanna fuck her!

SUNNY

Seriously, Dollar. You could break her by takin' all her money, her jewelry, and anything you want you could take it. But let her pimp know why you broke her and what she did to get broke.

DOLLAR BILL

Thanks for the lesson. But I still wanna fuck her!

Back on Sunset Blvd. in the strip club parking lot, Tiger and his wife are talking.

TIGER

Where the fuck you been? You lucky you my wife.

TIGERS WIFE

Tiger stop tripping.

TIGER

Where your wife-in-laws at?

TIGERS WIFE

Getting your trap money.

Another pimp (BIG BLACK) pulls into the parking lot driving a convertible mustang with two prostitutes, a white girl and a black girl. He parks, exits the vehicle and joins Tiger and his wife, giving Tiger dapps.

BIG BLACK

>What's up Tiger my nigga?

TIGER

>What's up Black. I see you got a new bitch. Not bad.

BIG BLACK

>I took that ho from a baseball cap wearin' tennis shoe pimp.

The black girl, hearing Tiger compliment her, smiles at Tiger from the back seat of the car.

BIG BLACK

>(To black girl)
>Bitch. Who the fuck you smilin' at ho!

BLACK GIRL

>At you daddy.

BIG BLACK

>Bring your ass here now bitch.

The black girl fearfully exits the vehicle and walks over to Big Black. Big Black grabs the girl, hitting, slapping and finally dragging her on the ground.

BIG BLACK

>You funky ass ho. Don't you ever disrespect me. You hear me bitch.

BLACK GIRL

>Ok! Ok! Stop, Black please, stop I'm sorry I'm sorry. Black Pleease!!

BIG BLACK

> I'll kill your ass ho! If I ever catch you "wreck less eye ballin'" another nigga again! Now get your ass up and go get my motha fuckin' money ho. (to white girl) You too bitch.

The black girl gets up off the ground, brushes herself off, still crying and runs across the street without looking back. The white girl jumps out of the car and obediently runs across the street carrying her tiny bag.

TIGERS WIFE

> (to Tiger)
> That niggas a beast.

BIG BLACK

> See Tiger. You gotta keep them hos' in line or they'll run all over you.

Big Black, looking across the street motions with his hands to another prostitute (PROSTITUTE 3). She looks over at him and staggers across the street.

BIG BLACK

> Bring your mother fuckin' ass here ho.

TIGER

> (to his wife)
> Is it just me or is that bitch high as a kite.

TIGERS WIFE

> That bitch is fucked up.

BIG BLACK

> Bitch you fucked up again?

PROSTITUTE 3

>I'm not high.

Big Black slaps her and she falls to the ground.

BIG BLACK

>The fuck you ain't bitch! I told you I don't work like that. How the fuck you gonna make my money. You can't even stand up straight. Get your ass in the car now before I fuck you up tramp!

Ho 3 staggers over to the Mustang and climbs into the back seat. Big Black follows behind her and gets in the car. Before he drives off he slaps her again.

Dollar Bill and Sunny are driving down Sunset Blvd. Tiger drives by in his car with his wife and two other hos'. Dollar Bill waves out his window getting Tiger's attention. Tiger, seeing Dollar Bill, makes a u-turn in the street. Dollar Bill pulls over to the side of the street and Tiger pulls up beside him.

TIGER

>What's up young player . . . holla at me.

TIGERS WIFE

>Hey girl, what's up Sunny? I haven't seen you in a while girlfriend. Where you been girl?

SUNNY

>Taking a break. I see you still rolling strong.

TIGERS WIFE

>You know it.

TIGER

Before I was rudely interrupted, what the fuck is this? A ho reunion? Damn. Yo Dollar, you got a dime piece in the car with you, young player.

DOLLAR BILL

Hey T baby, I need a cell phone, a bootleg one. Can you hook me up?

TIGER

Meet me tomorrow at the spot where we was rapping at earlier.

DOLLAR BILL

How much are they runnin' for?

TIGER

About a bill to a bill fifty. They last a long time too.

DOLLAR BILL

I'm there.

TIGERS WIFE

Bye Sunny. See ya on the track girl.

SUNNY

Ok girl. Bye, see ya later.

Tiger makes a u-turn and drives off in the direction he was headed originally. Dollar Bill pulls out continuing down Sunset Blvd.

SUNNY

I see you makin' the right connections.

Next morning. Dollar Bill is driving out of the Mc Donalds drive-thru, eating his breakfast. Looking all around, he notices three gorgeous, skimpily dressed girls walking towards a convertible Rolls Royce. A tall, well-built man with dreadlocks is holding the door open for them. They climb into the Rolls Royce, the man walks around the car, getting in the drivers side and they pull off.

Back inside the motel room Sunny is sprawled out on the bed, wearing a negligee watching T.V.

SUNNY

> Where you been?

DOLLAR BILL

> Getting us breakfast.

Dollar Bill hands her the bag of food, undresses and lays down next to Sunny in his boxers. Sunny begins eating

SUNNY

> Thanks you baby. Nobody ever brought me breakfast in bed. Where's your food?

DOLLAR BILL

> I ate mine in the car.

SUNNY

> Damn, you must have been hungry.

DOLLAR BILL

> I learned to eat fast in prison.

SUNNY

> I just heard on the news that they found a dead body in the alley last night, a man was shot to death.

DOLLAR BILL

No shit. That's fucked up. I'm gonna take my ass back to sleep.

Across town in the residential neighborhood of Beverly Hills, Tiger is conversing with a middle aged BUSINESSMAN who is clad in an expensive suit and tie. They are sitting outside in the backyard by the swimming pool of a luxurious mansion.

BUSINESSMAN

Where have you been hiding? I haven't seen you in a while.

TIGER

Been out of town getting my paper. You got somethin' for me?

BUSINESSMAN

Depends on what you want ... drugs, girls, money ... just talk to me.

TIGER

What's the 411 on the horns.

BUSINESSMAN

I have a few of them available. What's your preference and how many? You looking for flip phones, camera phones, walkie-talkie phones or just your ordinary plain jane?

TIGER

What the flip phones hittin' for?

BUSINESSMAN

I usually charge five hundred dollars with a one year connection guarantee. But for you Tiger, since I like you, and we been doing business together for a long time, just give me two-fifty.

Tiger reaches in his pocket, pulls out a roll of money and counts out two hundred and fifty dollars. He lays it on the table, then leans back in his chair.

TIGER

How's the wife and kids?

BUSINESSMAN

Spending my money like always. How's your wife?

TIGER

Makin' my money like always.

BUSINESSMAN

I could learn a few things from you Tiger.

TIGER

I'm up outa here. Gotta go pick up my phone.

Tiger and the businessman both stand up and shake hands, smiling. Tiger turns to leave.

BUSINESSMAN

You're forgetting something.

Tiger turns back around and the businessman hands him a key. Tiger, taking the key, leaves through the front door of the mansion, hops into a Mercedes Benz and drives off.

Back in Hollywood Tiger pulls into a gas station, parks by a pump and gets out. He enters the station and hands the key to the gas clerk, who in return hands him a cell phone.

TIGER

Give me twenty on number 1.

Tiger walks back to his car and begins pumping gas.

Night falls over the city, Dollar Bill and Sunny are driving down Sunset Blvd. He pulls the car over where a group of prostitutes are hanging out laughing and joking. Sunny jumps out and Dollar Bill pulls off. Further down the street he pulls into the strip club parking lot where many pimps are hanging out. Dollar Bill parks, exits the vehicle and walks over to Tiger.

DOLLAR BILL

What's up T baby. Talk to me.

TIGER

You in luck white boy. I got a hell of a deal for you. I know I told you a bill to a bill fifty, but I paid three hundred for a one year guaranteed connection. If it goes off you get your money back. You can't get that deal no where in this town for less than five hundred. If you don't want it that's cool too.

DOLLAR BILL

One year connection guarantee? Nigga I ain't no fool. I would have paid five hundred for it.

Dollar Bill pulls out a roll of bills, counts out three hundred dollars in twenties, hands them to Tiger in exchange for the phone.

TIGER

I ain't tryin' to make no money off you young player. I know you would have paid five hundred for it. But I like you, you keep it real. I'm just tryin' to let you get your pimp hand in the door.

DOLLAR BILL

> I feel you, businessman.

Down the street, two prostitutes (both all American looking white girls) are arguing with a trick. The trick (TRICK 2) grabs one of the prostitutes, (PROSTITUTE 4) around the shoulders. The other girl (PROSTITUTE 5) is watching.

PROSTITUTE 4

> You mother fuckin' bastard! You don't be disrespectin' me like that. Get your damn hands off me!

TRICK 2

> You mother fucking whore! Give me the god damned money.

Prostitute 5 jumps on the tricks' back and grabs him in a choke hold.

PROSTITUTE 5

> Get your mother fuckin' hands off of her. Grab his wallet, girl, grab his wallet.

The trick falls to his knees choking, and lets go of prostitute 4. He reaches in his waist band and pulls out a gun.

TRICK 2

> I'm gonna kill both you whores.

PROSTITUTE 4

> He got a gun! He got a gun! Help! Help!

Prostitute 4 runs off screaming. The trick elbows prostitute 5 in the gut, she folds to a crouching position, the wind knocked out of her. The trick now free, turns around and aims the gun at prostitute 5 and shoots her six times. Her body convulses as every shot hits her body.

TRICK 2

Bitch, all you had to do was give me your money. Stupid whore!

The trick runs down a side street and disappears with the gun in his hand. Traffic on Sunset Blvd. continues as normal. The prostitute lies bleeding on the street, no one stops to help.

Back in the parking lot of the strip club the other prostitute comes running across the street, almost getting hit by on coming traffic. She runs up to Tiger, gasping for breath.

PROSTITUTE 4

A trick just shot a ho! I think she's dead.

TIGER

Get the fuck in the car. Where my wife at?

PROSTITUTE 4

Up the street, the same way the trick ran.

Ho 4 runs to Tiger's car. Dollar Bill and Tiger each jump in their cars. and peel out of the parking lot, tires smoking and screeching. They both race up Sunset Blvd. towards the crime scene looking frantically around. Tiger spots his wife and girls on the other side of the street. He runs a red light and spins a u-turn ignoring oncoming cars. Screeching to a halt, his wife and all the girls jump in and Tiger speeds off down Highland away from Sunset Blvd.

Dollar Bill still racing down the street, passes Sunny up who is leaning on the window of a car. He slams on his brakes, backs up, tires screeching, then slams on his brakes again, pulling to a stop next to Sunny and the trick's car. The trick, frightened takes off, knocking Sunny to the ground.

DOLLAR BILL

> Get the fuck in the car now!

Sunny gets up, dazed, and jumps into the car, before she can close the door, Dollar Bill speeds off.

SUNNY

> What the fuck you doin' Dollar.? That was a hundred dollars! You trippin'? Have you lost your damn mind.

DOLLAR BILL

> You alright baby? I'm sorry girl. I just had to make sure you were alright first.

SUNNY

> What the fuck you talkin' about?

DOLLAR BILL

> A trick just shot a ho on the track. I had to get you off the street. Fuck the hundred dollars. We're done for the night.

SUNNY

> We don't have to be. We can go to the other track in the valley.

DOLLAR BILL

> What other track?

SUNNY

> Van Nuys. But stop by the motel, I gotta change my clothes.

DOLLAR BILL

> Let's make this shit happen.

Back at the motel parking lot, Dollar Bill is sitting in the car. Sunny is running down the stairs barefoot, still in her dirty clothes carrying a bag. She jumps in the car and strips naked changing into a pair of daisy duke shorts, a halter top and stripper shoes as they drive off.

Now in Van Nuys, Dollar Bills pulls into Fat Burger where several other pimps are hanging out and prostitutes are walking up and down the street. Sunny gets out of the car, attracting everyone's attention, even the other prostitutes are watching her as she walks up the track.

Dollar Bill walks inside Fat Burger. Another pimp (TOO-TALL) strikes up a conversation with Dollar Bill. Giving him dapps.

TOO-TALL

What's up Playboy? I'm Too-Tall. That's a fine little ho you got right there.

DOLLAR BILL

She make my money. I'm Dollar Bill.

TOO-TALL

Did you hear what happened on the track out there in Hollywood?

DOLLAR BILL

No, what happened?

TOO-TALL

A trick tried to rob a ho, then another ho came and tried to help her, then he shot one of the bitches, I heard about six times. And that bitch still alive!

DOLLAR BILL

No shit? Damn. Unbelievable.

TOO-TALL

> Hell yea. If that was my bitch I'd be scared to fuck with her. She like a cat with nine lives. I'd let that bitch go!

DOLLAR BILL

> That's some crazy shit man. Robbin' a ho.

Sunny enters the Fat Burger with the drink in her hand, walking by Dollar Bill and Too-Tall, and sits at a table by the window.

DOLLAR BILL

> Hold on for a minute Too-Tall.

Dollar Bill joins Sunny at the table and she hands him money. In the background cars are pulling up and driving off, prostitutes are walking by, hanging out and sometimes getting in and out of the cars.

SUNNY

> Here's a hundred dollars. I found it layin' on the ground out front. I need to take a break for a minute. I ain't feelin' so good.

DOLLAR BILL

> That's cool baby.

Too-Tall walks over to the table giving Dollar Bill dapps.

TOO-TALL

> I'm out.

DOLLAR BILL

> Peace out Too-Tall. Catch you on the track.

TOO-TALL

Keep them hos' on their toes and your money will be your reward.

Too-Tall walks out of Fat Burger.

SUNNY

Fuck Too-Tall and his bullshit. He ain't nothin' but a crack head. He get high with his hos'.

DOLLAR BILL

No shit? Dudes a base head?

SUNNY

Hell yea. Smoked out. He beat one of his hos' up cause the dope ran out.

DOLLAR BILL

I didn't know these pimps out here get high.

SUNNY

Yep. Some do, some don't. You can make a lot of money just sellin' dope to them and their hos'.

DOLLAR BILL

I can't sell the hos' shit. They ain't fuckin' with me, but you could.

SUNNY

Now you hearin' me. I can grab a date here and there and sell them dope on the side and we'll make even more money.

DOLLAR BILL

I like that shit. Let's vibrate up outa this mother fucker.

Back in the car, they turn off the 101 freeway onto Sunset Blvd, stopping at the next red light. Sunny points at a young black guy wearing baggy jeans, a basketball jersey, baseball cap, silver jewelry and tennis shoes. He is standing a few feet behind a poorly dressed ho, glaring suspiciously.

SUNNY

Dollar, look, look! See that fool right there? That's what you call a tennis shoe pimp.

DOLLAR BILL

What the fuck is a tennis shoe pimp?

SUNNY

Niggas' who be tryin' to be the man but they ain't shit. They don't respect the game. Most of 'em don't have a car and wear swap meet clothes. They can't afford gators, snakes, ostrich or lizards. They be lookin' so stupid. They ain't makin' no real money. They be fightin' with each other over their hos. Real pimps respect the game and would never fight over a ho.

The light changes and they pull off.

DOLLAR BILL

But he still pimpin'. He still got a ho, he makin' money?

SUNNY

That don't mean shit cause you take a hos' money. Any body can put a girl on the street and take what little money she make. Look at his ho! She's dirty, her hair ain't did, wearing a skirt with tennis shoes instead of stripper shoes. He dressed better than she is. A ho gotta dress better than her pimp, cause she the one makin' the money. When a ho ain't makin' no money the pimp gotta front the bill.

DOLLAR BILL

    What bill?

SUNNY

    A real pimp takes care of his ho. He pays her doctor
bills, feeds her, dresses her, puts a roof over her head,
protects her, bails her out of jail. That's what a real
pimp does.

DOLLAR BILL

    I'm glad I got gators.

SUNNY

    Seriously Dollar a tennis shoe pimp will fuck up your
reputation with the real players. Real hos' don't fuck
with tennis shoe pimps. I love you daddy. I'm not
tryin' to tell you how to run your shit but I've been
in the game all my life.

Several months later. Dollar Bill and Sunny are pulling into the Athletic
Club on Sunset Blvd. in a brand new $80,000.00 shiny black BMW.
They pull up in the valet parking and get out. Dollar Bill is dressed
in an all white Armani suit with black gator boots, matching belt,
diamond necklace, matching bracelet and diamond pinky ring. Sunny
is wearing a Versace mini dress with matching pumps, and diamond
studded necklace, bracelet and earrings. There is a long line waiting to
enter the club. Dollar Bill and Sunny walk arm in arm to the front of
the line. All eyes are on them as they walk up to the bouncer. Dollar
Bill reaches out to shake the bouncers hand, slipping him money.

DOLLAR BILL

    I'm Dollar Bill. I'm on the guest list.

The bouncer briefly glances at his list.

BOUNCER

>Dollar Bill, Dollar Bill. Here you go, have a good time.

DOLLAR BILL

>Thank you sir. And if you need anything at all just let me know. I got that.

The bouncer nods respectfully.

SUNNY

>Thank you.

They walk into the club as if they own the place, immediately becoming the center of attention. Going directly to the crowded dance floor, smiling and laughing, they begin dancing provocatively. Leaving the dance floor a few moments later, still smiling and holding hands like newlyweds, they walk over to an empty booth.

DOLLAR BILL

>After you my love.

SUNNY

>You are such a gentleman Dollar. That's why I love you.

Sunny sits down elegantly and Dollar bill slides in beside her.

SUNNY

>Baby, look around you. You gettin' mad respect in here. You earned your pimpin' rights. Even on the track, hos' talkin', pimps talkin', you large baby.

A sexy waitress arrives at the booth, leaning over to expose her cleavage.

WAITRESS

>Can I get you something to drink?

SUNNY

I'll have a shot of Convasia, please.

DOLLAR BILL

And I'll have a bottled water.

WAITRESS

Will that be all?

DOLLAR BILL

Yes, thank you.

Waitress walks away. Across the room Tiger is standing by the bar with his wife and a few of his girls.

DOLLAR BILL

Sunny, I'm gonna holla at Tiger for a minute. I'll be right back.

He walks across the room to join Tiger at the bar, giving him dapps.

DOLLAR BILL

What's up big time?

TIGER

Dollar, what's up baby? How you hangin'?

DOLLAR BILL

Not with a rope, I hope.

TIGER

White boy got jokes. Ok, ok.

DOLLAR BILL

Just payin' my respects. What you drinkin'? (cont.)

(to BARTENDER) Yo. A round of drinks for my friends here. Serve them whatever they want. Keep the change.

Dollar Bill tosses a hundred dollar bill on the bar.

TIGER

> I've met a lot of real players in my life, but you got class, Dollar. Even if you are a white boy.

DOLLAR BILL

> I grew up in a black neighborhood, all my boys are black. I know how you people think.

Dollar Bill and Tiger laugh together and give each other dapps.

TIGER

> Fuck you Dollar.

DOLLAR BILL

> Remember now, white boy do got jokes. See ya on the track.

Dollar Bill walks back to his booth where Sunny is waiting with their drinks.

DOLLAR BILL

> There's some bad bitches up in this motha fucka

SUNNY.

> See that nigga over there who just walked in, the Jamaican dude? That's JUMBO, he a millionaire pimp.

Strutting through the club is a large Jamaican, decked out in a red designer suit and diamonds, with long dreadlocks. He is surrounded by girls; black, white Asian and Mexican, all attractive and scantily dressed.

DOLLAR BILL

I've seen him before. I hear he got more bitches than any pimp on the track.

SUNNY

No shit. That's why we can't make as much money as we should be makin'. Not sayin' we hurtin' but if we take him and his hos' out of the box, we'd really be ballin'!

DOLLAR BILL

So what the fuck you tryin' to say Sunny?

SUNNY

We kill that motha fucka!

DOLLAR BILL

Bitch! I ain't goin' to jail for killin' some motha fuckin' pimp! Ho, you drinkin' too much motha fuckin' Convasia.

SUNNY

Dollar, do you wanna be rich? Or is this as far as you wanna go with yours? Cause I want it all! Who brought you into this game when you didn't have shit? Everything I do is for you. I love you, Dollar. And if that means I have to kill to give you more, then call me Jack the Ripper. There's nothin' I wouldn't do for you.

DOLLAR BILL

Fuck it. Let's do this shit.

SUNNY

That's what I'm talkin' about, baby. Give me a kiss.

Dollar Bill leans over and gives her a kiss.

SUNNY

> I know where he eat at every Friday night.

DOLLAR BILL

> Shut the fuck up for a minute. I run this shit here, you don't run shit. I'll do the thinking!.

SUNNY

> I'm sorry baby.

Back inside their lavish, expensively decorated 2000 sq. ft. condo, Dollar Bill and Sunny are relaxing on the couch.

DOLLAR BILL

> Ok, so tell me where Jumbo eats every Friday night.

SUNNY

> He eats alone at the Dennys on Sunset every Friday night, while his hos' are working.

DOLLAR BILL

> Hold on now. There is two Dennys on Sunset. Which one?

SUNNY

> The one by the 101 freeway where we always eat.

DOLLAR BILL

> That work. I like the way the parking lot's set up in the back. Its secluded and dark with more than one escape route.

SUNNY

> You took the words right outa my mouth.

DOLLAR BILL

So you tellin' me a nigga that rich eat at Dennys every fuckin' week? Unbelievable.

SUNNY

Everybody knows they got good food and the best service.

DOLLAR BILL

Ok. This is what we gonna do. We wait for him to come out of the restaurant and then . . .

Next Friday night. Dollar Bill and Sunny are sitting and waiting inside Sunny's car at the parking lot of Dennys. They are parked next to the convertible Rolls Royce.

DOLLAR BILL

Bitch, you ready to do this shit?

SUNNY

You know it.

DOLLAR BILL

I can't believe I'm out here in a motha fuckin' Dennys parking lot with a ho about to kill a pimp over some bread. Unbelievable.

SUNNY

Dollar, here he come. Get down!

Dollar ducks down inside the car. Sunny jumps out of the car and walks over to the Rolls Royce. As Jumbo turns the corner he sees Sunny standing next to his car, smiling invitingly at him. He walks over to her.

JUMBO

> Bitch, you must be ready to choose a real player or you just a stupid ho. Which one is it?

SUNNY

> I been ready to choose and now I'm choosin'.

JUMBO

> Get in the car ho.

SUNNY

> Ok daddy.

Jumbo gets in his car as Sunny opens the passenger side door and joins him. They drive off together down Sunset Blvd. Dollar, slowly creeps behind them in Sunny's car, keeping his distance.

JUMBO

> So who's your pimp ho?

SUNNY

> He's in jail, so you are now.

JUMBO

> Bout time you finally came to your senses. So maybe you not a stupid ho after all. You got nice lips.

SUNNY

> And I give a hell of a blow job. Better than any ho you ever had.

JUMBO

> Is that right?

SUNNY

> That's right, daddy. Pull down one of these side streets and let your new bitch show you what she made of.

Jumbo turns down a dark, side street off of Sunset Blvd. and parks. Dollar Bill cuts off his lights before he turns the corner, he pulls over and parks several cars behind them.

JUMBO

> Ok ho. You got a lot of mouth for such a little bitch. Let's see if your lips can even fit around my Jumbo dick.

Sunny unzips Jumbo's pants exposing his dick and she begins sucking it. Dollar Bill is creeping up behind them, crouched below the cars, with a baseball bat in his hand. He cracks Jumbo over the head repeatedly, blood and tissue splattering everywhere. Jumbo slumps over the steering wheel motionless. Sunny jumps up watching Dollar Bill, then looking back at Jumbo's dick.

SUNNY

> Damn, now I see why they call you Jumbo.

DOLLAR BILL

> Bitch, stop fuckin' around.

SUNNY

> Sorry baby.

DOLLAR BILL

> Bitch, you sure you never killed nobody before?

SUNNY

> I never trusted anyone before.

DOLLAR BILL

> Help me put this big motha fucka in the back seat.

Dollar Bill and Sunny struggle with the dead body pulling it into the back seat.

DOLLAR BILL

> Go down the street and get the car. The keys are still in the ignition. Then follow me.

Dollar Bill jumps into the drivers seat pulling out slowly. Sunny runs down the street and jumps into her car, following behind Dollar Bill. They drive up into the Hollywood Hills to a deserted field. Dollar Bill pulls over and stops, and Sunny comes to a stop a few yards behind him. They get out of the cars and Sunny runs over to Dollar Bill.

DOLLAR BILL

> Go get the gas can out of the trunk.

Sunny runs back to her car, opens the trunk retrieving the gas can, slams the trunk shut, then runs back to Dollar Bill carrying the gas can.

SUNNY

> Now what you want me to do?

DOLLAR BILL

> Bitch, now you pour the gas all over Jumbo and his car, shit. That's what the fuck you can do! And don't forget to leave a gas line trail so you don't blow yourself up when you light the bitch.

SUNNY

> You sure you ain't killed nobody before.

DOLLAR BILL

> Bitch, shut the fuck up and pour the gas.

Sunny pours the gas all over the car and Jumbo. Dollar Bill returns to Sunny's car and watches from the drivers seat. Sunny carefully makes a gas trail about two car lengths away from her car. She lights up a match, drops it on the trail, and runs away from the flames jumping back in the car out of breath. They both watch as the flames suddenly light up the sky like daytime, before they drive off.

Back inside their condo Dollar Bill and Sunny strip down naked, putting all their clothes and shoes inside a big, round, metal wash bucket. They place it inside the shower, pouring lighter fluid over the clothes, then setting them on fire. They go to the other bathroom and shower together.

DOLLAR BILL

> We gotta go to work now and act normal.

SUNNY

> Where did you put the dope at?

DOLLAR BILL

> It's in the safe.

Sunny, hurriedly jumps from the shower grabbing a towel, drying off as she runs back into the other bathroom. She drops the towel on the floor and retrieves the wash bucket with the now burnt ashes. She walks quickly into the kitchen and dumps the ashes into a lined trash can, then pulls out the bag and securely ties it. Returning to the master bedroom, Dollar Bill is already dressed. Sunny rushes to her closet, grabbing a red mini dress and pulling it over her head. The safe door is ajar.

DOLLAR BILL

> I already got the dope out of the safe. Did you dump the bucket of ashes?

SUNNY

> Yes I did.

DOLLAR BILL

> Meet me outside. I'll be waiting in the BMW. Lock everything up.

Dollar Bill walks calmly out of the bedroom into the kitchen and grabs the trash bag tied up containing the ashes. He exits the condo, walks downstairs, getting into his car while placing the trash bag in the back seat. Waiting in the car with the motor running he calls Sunny. Inside the condo the phone rings in the bedroom four times. Sunny picks up the phone.

SUNNY

> Yo.

DOLLAR BILL

> What's takin' you so long girl, let's go! Shit.

Sunny puts on her shoes as she hurries down the stairs to the waiting car.

Turning into a back alley from Sunset Blvd, Dollar Bill parks next to a dumpster. He jumps out of the car, grabs the trash bag from the back seat, tears it open and sprinkles the ashes into the dumpster. He throws the bag in last, then jumps back in his car and takes off back to Sunset Blvd, pulling over by the other Dennys.

SUNNY

> Sorry I took so long baby, I couldn't find my other red shoe.

Dollar smiles at Sunny

DOLLAR BILL

> I must really love your ass, girl! Killin' motha fucka' and shit! Are you scared?

SUNNY

No, I feel great.

DOLLAR BILL

Call me if you need anything.

SUNNY

I will. Love you.

DOLLAR BILL

Wait. You're forgetting everything. Open the glove box and get the forty dollars, the condoms, and the dope. You sure you ok?

SUNNY

Don't worry. I'm ok. How much is my quota tonight?

DOLLAR BILL

Three hundred dollars. Don't kill yourself now.

SUNNY

Fuck you Dollar.

Sunny gets out of the car and Dollar Bill drives off. As Sunny walks up the street a prostitute (LISA) calls to her.

LISA

Sunny!!

Sunny stops and turns around in the direction of the voice. Lisa walks up to her.

LISA

Hey girl, you got somethin'?

SUNNY

What you want Lisa? You still owe me ten dollars.

LISA

I got your money girl, don't trip.

SUNNY

Bitch I never trip. Where my ten dollars at. I gotta pay my nigga just like you do.

LISA

Can I pay you later Sunny? If Too-Tall don't get all his money he gonna kick my ass tonight.

SUNNY

Ho, that ain't my problem. If you wasn't out here smokin' with the nigga you wouldn't be getting' your ass beat. Bitch what you want?

LISA

Gimme a forty piece.

Sunny reaches in her bra and pulls out a bag of dope. Reaching in the bag, she pulls out a small rock and hands it to Lisa.

LISA

Thanks Sunny. Here's fifty. Dollars. You gonna be around later on tonight in case I need somethin' else?

SUNNY

I don't know. Bye Lisa.

Lisa runs back across the street joining a group of prostitutes.

Same night. In Hollywood Hills at the deserted field are several police cars. A swarm of police officers and news media wander around as a

DETECTIVE examines what is left of Jumbo's charred body inside the burnt Rolls Royce.

DETECTIVE

So what do we have here officer?

POLICE 2

We have one burnt body. I ran the plates on the vehicle and they belong to a Charles Kimble, black male, age 33, address 455 Beverly Rd. in Beverly Hills.

DETECTIVE

God damn! That's Jumbo!

POLICE 2

Who?

DETECTIVE

Jumbo. He's a pimp. I've been trying to put his ass away for years. His family is so god damned rich, every time I arrest him, they comes to his rescue, throwing around their millions with their big shot attorneys and the cases somehow just disappear.

POLICE 2

So what do you want us to do now?

DETECTIVE

Collect every last trace piece of evidence you can find. I don't care if it's dog shit on the ground, I want that too! Cause the man didn't burn himself up!

POLICE 2

Yes sir detective. (to news media) Hey!! Get the fuck away from the crime scene!! Damn reporters!

Back on Sunset Blvd. at the strip club parking lot, Dollar Bill is talking to Tiger.

TIGER

> It's slow out here tonight. I'm about to call it a night.

DOLLAR BILL

> That don't sound like a bad idea. My bitch been out here since ten o'clock and she only made two hundred dollars.

Dollar Bill's cell phone rings.

DOLLAR BILL

> Yo. What's up?

SUNNY

> Hey baby. Come pick up some money. I got too much on me.

DOLLAR BILL

> Where you at?

SUNNY

> On a pay phone by the other Dennys next to the 101 freeway. Are you at the parking lot? If you are, I'm walkin' up towards you.

DOLLAR BILL

> I'm on my way. (to Tiger) I'm out.

Walking through the door of their condo, Sunny notices the news on T.V. with Jumbo's picture across the screen.

SUNNY

> Dollar, look, look! They talkin' about Jumbo!

Dollar Bill and Sunny plop down on the couch with their eyes glued to the T.V.

DOLLAR BILL

Turn it up!

Sunny grabs the remote control and turns up the volume.

TV NEWS

'Was this a robbery gone bad? Can you tell us what happened here?

DETECTIVE

We don't know yet exactly what happened here. We suspect it may have been a drug deal gone bad. But the victim was also a very high profile pimp so we will be questioning all of the prostitutes who worked for him. No one is being ruled out as a suspect yet.

TV NEWS

So tell us Detective, what is your next step? How do you plan to catch the person or persons responsible for committing this horrific crime?

DETECTIVE

I'm sorry I can't disclose any more information at this time.

SUNNY

See baby. Jumbo was a fucked up nigga. Fuck him.

DOLLAR BILL

No sweat off my balls. Fuck him. Let's go get some breakfast.

Dollar Bill and Sunny get out of the car at Dennys and walk into the restaurant. A beautiful white girl (INDIO) with long jet black hair is walking in just ahead of them.

DOLLAR BILL

>(to Indio)
>Hey sexy! Don't I know you?

INDIO

>I know who you are. You're Dollar Bill.

HOSTESS

>How many? Smoking or non-smoking?

DOLLAR BILL

>Three of us, and non smoking please.

HOSTESS

>Right this way, please.

The hostess, a tall athletic built Hispanic girl, leads the way to a corner booth. Sunny slides in first, Dollar Bill stands back politely letting Indio slide in next to Sunny. Dollar Bill slides in last next to Indio, placing her in the middle.

HOSTESS

>I'll be right back to take your order.

Dollar Bill, Sunny, and Indio watch her walk away appreciatively.

DOLLAR BILL

>This is my girl, Sunny.

SUNNY

>Hi girl. You're beautiful. What's your name?

INDIO

Indio.

SUNNY

I love your hair. You should let me do it for you sometime.

DOLLAR BILL

So who do you work for?

INDIO

I work for D D.

DOLLAR BILL

D D?

INDIO

Yea.

DOLLAR BILL

That tennis shoe bum? I know you about to choose.

INDIO

He is a fuckin' loser.

DOLLAR BILL

Look how he got you dressin'. You're beautiful. You should be laced the fuck up, shinin' bright baby. Look at my girl, Sunny. She's beautiful too. She don't dress in nothin' but the best.

INDIO

She is beautiful. I like everything about her.

DOLLAR BILL

My phone is in my hand, just give me the number and I'll make that call.

INDIO

I've been wanting to be on your team for a long time. I just didn't know how. 555-4108.

Dollar Bill dials the number. Sunny happily hugs Indio.

SUNNY

Welcome to the family! I've been wanting a wife-in-law. I know D.D ain't gonna give you your shit, so we'll go shopping. And we're about the same size so you can wear anything of mine you want. And bitch, I wear Versace and Gucci.

D.D.

Hello.

DOLLAR BILL

Yo, what's up pimpin'?

D.D.

Who the fuck is this?

DOLLAR BILL

Dollar Bill baby.

D.D.

Oh shit. What's up Dollar Bill? What's goin' on player?

DOLLAR BILL

Your girl Indio, she choose me pimpin' You know the game.

D.D.

Fuck you Dollar Bill! You a Bitch! You ain't shit!

DOLLAR BILL

See ya!

Dollar Bill, smiling, hangs up in his face.

SUNNY

What did he say Dollar?

DOLLAR BILL

He said I ain't shit, fuck me and called me a bitch.

SUNNY

See I told you Dollar about those tennis shoe pimps.
They don't respect the game.

INDIO

Can I order somethin' to eat Dollar.

DOLLAR BILL

You part of the family now girl. Say what you want,
order what you want. I don't give a fuck.

SUNNY

Girl he mean that shit, literally. So order up. We don't
want no hungry hos'!

The hostess returns to the booth, placing three glasses of water on the
table.

HOSTESS

Ready to order?

DOLLAR BILL

Lady's first.

SUNNY

Since you're the special one today Indio, you order first.

INDIO

Thank you Sunny. Can I have steak and eggs, white toast, hash browns, a small fruit salad, chocolate cake, and a large glass of orange juice with ice.

HOSTESS

(to Sunny)

And you?

SUNNY

I want the same thing she havin'.

DOLLAR BILL

Me too.

HOSTESS

Your food will be right out.

Hostess walks off.

SUNNY

Damn Indio, you can eat girl. I know I ain't gonna eat all this food. It just sounds good.

INDIO

D.D. never took us out to a restaurant to eat. We ate cold sandwiches and McDonalds at the motel every day.

DOLLAR BILL

Damn. We eat out all the time. I don't even think Sunny can cook cause she damn sure never cooked for me.

SUNNY

Fuck you nigga. I don't need to cook, I got good pussy.

Indio tenses up, leaning way back in her seat, glancing nervously back and forth between Sunny and Dollar Bill.

DOLLAR BILL

(to Indio)
What's wrong girl? Look like you seen a ghost.

INDIO

I was just positioning myself.

DOLLAR BILL

Fo what?

INDIO

I was just waitin' for you to smack her.

DOLLAR BILL

Now why would I do that?

INDIO

For the way she cussed at you.

SUNNY

Listen girl, Dollar don't beat me, he don't smack me, he don't lay a hand on me. You don't never have to worry about that no matter how much you pis him off. His number one rule is "if he need to hit you, he don't want you."

DOLLAR BILL

No, that's rule number 2. Rule number one is "Never underestimate a woman."

INDIO

I would have got my ass kicked if I said fuck you to D.D. I haven't felt this happy in years. I already feel like family.

Hostess returns and places their food on the table.

HOSTESS

Here you go.

DOLLAR BILL

(to hostess)
Why don't you sit down and have breakfast with us, my treat.

HOSTESS

You tryin' to get me fired?

DOLLAR BILL

If that happens I guess I'll have to take care of you.

HOSTESS

Here comes my boss. I have to go.

She looks nervously over her shoulder at her boss glaring in their direction and turns and walks away. Everyone begins eating heartily.

DOLLAR BILL

    I know I can crack that bitch easy. I'm Dollar motha fuckin' Bill baby.

INDIO

    I can even crack that bitch.

DOLLAR BILL

    Fuck you Indio.

INDIO

    No, for real, if a woman is smilin' and lookin' at a man like that, she can be cracked. Unless the man fuck it up. Men are so stupid. They talk themselves right out of pussy all the time and they don't even know it.

Indio and Sunny laugh together and give each other dapps. Dollar Bill watches and laughs with them.

SUNNY

    She got you on that one Dollar.

DOLLAR BILL

    Unbelievable.

Dollar Bill raises his hand motioning to the hostess. She returns to the booth.

HOSTESS

    May I help you?

DOLLAR BILL

    You already have, sexy.

HOSTESS

    And how have I done that?

DOLLAR BILL

Just for bein' born.

HOSTESS

I see you got jokes.

DOLLAR BILL

That's the second time in my career I was told that. Maybe I should change careers and become a comedian.

HOSTESS

What is your career?

DOLLAR BILL

I'm an investor.

HOSTESS

So what do you invest in

DOLLAR BILL

I invest women's money

HOSTESS

So you're a pimp.

DOLLAR BILL

Pimp is such a harsh and brutal word. I prefer to call myself an investor. Women work hard for their money. They choose me to invest it for them so they don't have any worries. I pay their rent, I pay their medical bills, I buy their clothes and make-up, I feed them, I provide them security and transportation. I love and respect my women, I never lay a hand on them. I consider it a privilege to take care of women and their money. You're beautiful, why are you working here anyway? You could make a lot of money on the track.

HOSTESS

I work here to pay my bills.

Indio and Sunny watching Dollar Bill talk to the Hostess with amusement.

DOLLAR BILL

If you worked for me, you wouldn't have bills, worries or stress. You'd have fringe benefits and paid vacations.

HOSTESS

It makes sense the way you explain it.

DOLLAR BILL

How much do you make here? About six dollars an hour plus tips working eight hours a day, five days a week. After taxes you probably take home less than three hundred a week. Is that about right?

HOSTESS

That's about right.

DOLLAR BILL

You could make three hundred a night or more working for me. That's a lot of money, ain't it? Give me your pen.

The hostess reaches into her apron, pulls out a pen and hands it to Dollar Bill. Dollar Bill scribbles on a napkin and hands it to her.

DOLLAR BILL

Here's my number. Call me anytime, sexy.

HOSTESS

I'll think about it. By the way, keep the pen.

She smiles as she turns and walks away.

INDIO

Damn you are good. She even forgot all about the bill!

SUNNY

I felt like I was watching a stage play. Dollar you so full of shit. But in all reality, everything you told her was the truth.

DOLLAR BILL

Let's get the fuck up out of here.

SUNNY

Dollar, take us to the movies today. That'd be fun.

INDIO

Yea, Dollar Take us to the movies today. I haven't seen a movie in years.

DOLLAR BILL

I can do that for my ladies. Let's roll.

Dollar slides out of the booth, then steps back and waits while Indio slides out second and Sonny slides out last. Dollar Bill reaches into his pocket, pulling out a large roll of money, selects a one hundred dollar bill and tosses it on the table.

Back inside the condo Indio is walking around the living room, looking all around her, with wide-eyed wonder. Dollar and Sunny watch her smiling, like proud parents. Sunny then walks into the master bedroom to the closet and strips naked. Dollar follows her into the room and reclines on a chair.

SUNNY

Indio, come here girl!

Indio enters the master bedroom and joins Sunny in the closet.

SUNNY

Here girl, try this dress on. It's about your size.

INDIO

Oooh girl that's beautiful!

Indio lets her dress fall off revealing her naked body, looking at Sunny up and down from head to toe, licking her lips. She reaches over and grabs Sunny around the waist, kissing her deep, hard and passionately, like a man kisses a woman. Sunny places her hands on Indio's face, returning the kiss. Indio pulls Sunny over to the bed, still kissing her, then pushes her down on the bed roughly. She begins caressing her body everywhere, Dollar is looking on, smiling contentedly. Indio moves her mouth to Sunny's nipples sucking one and then the other. Sunny is moaning in pleasure while Indio moves her lips down between Sunny's legs and begins sucking on her hungrily. Sunny then sits up and rolls Indio over onto her stomach, kissing her slowly, from her neck to her ass, while Indio moans in delight.

SUNNY

You're so beautiful. How'd you know I like girls?

INDIO

A real woman knows.

DOLLAR BILL

My big dick sure is real hard right now.

INDIO

You like this shit don't you Dolllar?

DOLLAR BILL

What man wouldn't enjoy watching two beautiful woman fucking

INDIO

Come here Dollar baby. Bring your big, hard dick over here.

Dollar Bill gets up off the chair and joins them on the bed, stripping off all his clothes. He climbs on top of Indio, kissing her while Sunny embraces him from behind, rubbing her breasts on his back and kissing his neck. Dollar Bill penetrates Indio with deep, hard strokes. Suddenly the doorbell rings loudly, startling Sunny and Dollar Bill. Sunny freezes as Dollar Bill jumps up, grabbing his boxer shorts and pulling them on hastily.

DOLLAR BILL

Oh shit!

INDIO

I'll get it, Dollar, just relax.

DOLLAR BILL

No! You two get ready so we can go to the movies.

SUNNY

Come on Indio, let's get ready, fore we be in bed all day fucking.

Dollar Bill is walking back into the living room towards the front door. He checks through the peep-hole then cautiously opens the front door. A nerdy looking man, (LLOYD) wearing thick lenses, is standing in the doorway, smiling, with a coffee cup in his hand

Dollar Bill

DOLLAR BILL

What the fuck you want this time, Lloyd?

LLOYD

Sorry for bothering you again, Dollar. Can I borrow some coffee from you, dude?

DOLLAR BILL

Damn Lloyd, hold on man. You fucking up my pussy

Dollar Bill snatches the coffee cup from Lloyd's hand and slams the door in his face. He walks into the kitchen, pausing, then reaches into the cabinet grabbing an unopened 10lb can of coffee. With the cup in one hand and the can of coffee in the other, he returns to the door. and opens the door awkwardly.

DOLLAR BILL

Here's your cup Take the can. Do you want anything else, Lloyd? Do you want to come have dinner tonight, Lloyd? Do you want to come fuck my girl, Lloyd? What you want, Lloyd?

LLOYD

Hey Dollar, that would be fucking awesome man. I'd love to come fuck your girl.

Dollar Bill slams the door in his face, walking away mumbling to himself. He walks back through the bedroom, into the bathroom

DOLLAR BILL

Unbelievable.

He can see the girls through the shower window, showering and singing, a song by the Isley Brothers.

SUNNY & INDIO

> Drifting on a memory, ooh, ooh, ooh, there's no place I'd rather be than with you . . . well, loving you . . . well, well, well. Day will make the way for light, all we need is candlelight and a song . . . yea, soft and long . . . well, well, well.

Dollar Bill strips out of his boxers and joins the singing girls in the shower.

DOLLAR BILL

> I'm glad the concert started without me. I thought I was gonna' be the back up singer.

Sunny and Indio look at each other and begin laughing.

SUNNY

> (to Dollar)
> Who was that at the door?

DOLLAR BILL

> Lloyd's faggot ass begging for some coffee again. So I gave his ass the whole can.

Same day. Outside of the Universal Studio theaters, Dollar Bill, Sunny and Indio are looking at the list of movies playing.

DOLLAR BILL

> What do you 'all want to watch?

INDIO

> Let's watch an action flick.

SUNNY

> Ooh, that sounds good.

DOLLAR BILL

> Well an action flick we shall see. All in favor, raise
> your hand.

All three raise their hands and laugh. Walking into the theater, loaded
down with popcorns, candy bars and drinks, they choose seats in the
middle of the theater. Taking their seats they begin devouring the
snacks,

DOLLAR BILL

> One day they're gonna make a movie about me called
> "Dollar Bill".

INDIO

> That would be a great movie . . . about you investing
> all the girls money

SUNNY

> Girl, you so crazy. Shhh be quiet, the movies about
> to come on

The lights fade. One by one their heads begin to droop, the snacks are
forgotten and within minutes they are all sound asleep on each others
shoulders.

The movie ends, the lights come up, people begin exiting the theater.
Sunny awakens first, waking Dollar Bill and then Indio.

SUNNY

> Damn, we was all knocked out after being up all night.

DOLLAR BILL

> What time is it?

INDIO

> Shit. It's like 6:30. We gotta get ready for work.

DOLLAR BILL

Let's vibrate ourselves up outa this mother fucker.

They all stand up in unison and exit the theater. Walking through the lobby, Sunny says . . .

SUNNY

I have to go to the bathroom, baby

INDIO

Me too, girl. I was dreaming that I had to pee.

Sunny and Indio enter into the bathroom, Dollar waits outside. A MIDGET, dressed in checkered pants and a flowered shirt approaches Dollar Bill . . .

MIDGET

Hey bud. Nice looking chicks, which one is yours so I can holler at the other one.

DOLLAR BILL

Man, get the fuck out of here with your little ass. You couldn't even reach the pussy.

MIDGET

Fuck you then you wanna-be pimp.

The midget jumps towards Dollar Bill with his fists clenched and raised. A beautiful, blonde, classy, tall girl exits the bathroom, Dollar forgets the midget, staring at her.

DOLLAR BILL

(to the girl)

Hey sexy.

She gives him a disgusted look, then smiles at the midget, grabbing his hand as they walk off together. The midget glances over his shoulder and gives Dollar Bill the middle finger while sticking out his tongue.

The girls exit the bathroom together holding hands, Dollar Bill is still looking in disbelief at the midget and the girl walking off.

SUNNY

What's wrong Dollar?

DOLLAR BILL

I can't believe this shit. I got dissed by a midget. What is this world coming to.

INDIO

You mean the movie star Dollar Bill got dissed by a midget. Unbelievable.

Back inside the condo in the master bedroom, Dollar Bill is reclining on his chair watching T.V, and glancing impatiently at the girls. He is already dressed, wearing a red silk shirt, white slacks, with red ostrich boots and matching belt. On the bed is a mountain of clothes. The girls are pulling clothes from the closet, trying them on and off, throwing them on the bed, giggling and modeling for each other.

DOLLAR BILL

God damn ya'all. Ya'all not at the fuckin' Beverly Center. Ya'all tried on at least twenty god damned outfits already. We got to roll up outa here.

SUNNY

We're almost ready, we coming. (to Indio) How you like this one?

INDIO

> Damn girl, that's hot. Wear that one. How you like this one?

DOLLAR BILL

> Damn Indio, that's hot. Wear that one.

INDIO

> I'm sorry, Dollar, we coming right now.

The girls pulling out accessories finish dressing rapidly. Indio is wearing a long, black and white, checkered dress split up both sides to her thighs, with clear rhinestone stripper shoes. Sunny is dressed in a canary yellow mini dress with matching stripper shoes.

SUNNY & INDIO

> Ok, we ready, we ready.

DOLLAR BILL

> You two are stunning!

INDIO

> Us women like hearing shit like that. That might just get you some pussy.

Dollar Bill stands up heading to the front door as the girls follow.

SUNNY

> Oh shit, I forgot the dope.

DOLLAR BILL

> We'll meet you in the car.

Dollar Bill and Indio walk out the front door leaving it open behind them. Sunny enters the bedroom, opening the safe and grabbing the bag of dope. She hurries out the front door and locks the bottom lock pulling the door shut behind her. Walking rapidly down the stairs to the BMW where Dollar Bill and Indio are waiting in the car with the motor running and headlights on. Sunny jumps in and they pull off into the night.

Back on Sunset Blvd. Dollar Bill and his girls are slowly cruising up the street, looking around at the other prostitutes running up to the cars as they pull over, then jumping in and driving off with their dates. Dollar Bill finally turns down a side street and pulls over and stops.

DOLLAR BILL

Here's some money for work, be careful, call me if you need me.

Sunny takes the money and jumps out of the car, walking back towards Sunset Blvd. Dollar Bill drives off. Indio climbs over into the front seat. Doll Bill drives around the corner, pulling over just before Sunset Blvd. Dollar Bill hands Indio some money and a piece of paper.

DOLLAR BILL

The forty dollars is for emergencies and so you can't be arrested for loitering by the police. I wrote my number on the paper if you need anything. Open the glove box and get out some condoms.

INDIO

Damn. You so prepared, Dollar. You must've been a boy scout.

DOLLAR BILL

Not exactly. I just always have a plan and a back up. And tell Sunny to show you where all the spots are to take your tricks, so we always know where to find you when you have a date. And if the trick don't want to go, fuck him. Now go get my trap money bitch.

Indio jumps out of the car. Dollar bill drives off and turns onto Sunset Blvd. He spots Sunny already getting into a car. Dollar continues driving and turns down another side street, stopping, glances up the alley, and pulls off. He drives back to Sunset Blvd. and turns down a different alley, slowly cruising, till he spots the car that picked up Sunny. Turning off his lights he pulls over and parks, watching the trick on top of Sunny fucking her fast while the car rocked from side to side.

Minutes later, Sunny jumps out of the car, as it pulls off. Dollar bill turns the car on, and Sunny jumps in as Dollar Bill pulls off.

SUNNY

> Here baby, I got a hundred dollars out of that trick.

DOLLAR BILL

> Put it in the glove box. That was a quick hundred dollars. I want you to show Indio all the spots we work out of, as soon as possible.

Dollar Bill drives around the corner, pulling over as Sunny gets out again. He drives off. back to Sunset Blvd., where he sees Indio getting into a car. Keeping his distance, he follows behind the car. The car turns down a side street and pulls over and parks. Dollar Bill drives past them, and drives around the block, turning off his headlights before he returns to the street where Indio is in the parked car. Creeping he pulls over and parks behind the car, through the back window he can see Indio riding the trick (TRICK 4) Inside the car where Indio and the trick are still in action . . .

INDIO

> Ooh daddy! Fuck me harder, harder! Damn you got a big dick, daddy!

TRICK 4

> Ride that white horse, bitch! Damn you got some good pussy, ho!

INDIO

> Ooh daddy, I'm about to come . . . Ok, ok, right there . . . ooooh daddy! I'm comin"! Damn!

Indio jumps off of the trick.

TRICK 4

> Where you going? I didn't come yet, ho.

INDIO

> Oh I'm so sorry. But mine sure felt good.

Indio climbs back on top of the trick and begins riding him again. Dollar Bill is still watching them, looking at his watch, obviously growing impatient. Finally Indio jumps out of the trick's car, pulling down her dress. Dollar Bill flicks the headlights, Indio seeing him, jumps into his car, grinning. Dollar Bill drives off back to Sunset Blvd. the cell phone rings

DOLLAR BILL

> Yo.

SUNNY

> It's me. Come pick up some money. Where's Indio? I was looking for her.

DOLLAR BILL

> She's here with me. She just got off a date. Where you at?

SUNNY

> I'm at the 7-11, the one closest to the strip club going east.

DOLLAR BILL

> Actually I'm headed towards your way now. See you in a minute. Bye. (to Indio) Damn bitch, you been with that motha fucka about forty minutes. How much money he give you?

INDIO

> Here, baby. It's forty dollars. I'm sorry Dollar.

DOLLAR BILL

> Put the money in the glove box.

Dollar Bill pulls over into the 7-11 and parks. in front of the door. Sunny is walking out of the store drinking a juice, and seeing the car, she jumps in.

SUNNY

> Here Dollar. I put your money in the glove box, it's a hundred and seventy five dollars. Hey Indio.

INDIO

> Hey girl, you gotta show me where the working spots are.

DOLLAR BILL

> I'm gonna leave both you'all hos' here. Now get the fuck out and get my trap money.

SUNNY & INDIO

> Ok, alright.

DOLLAR BILL

> Indio, if you know any girls on the track that want to buy dope, send them to Sunny.

INDIO

Yes sir.

Both of the girls get out of the car, walking off together. Indio squeezes Sunny's ass as they walk down the street. Immediately a car pulls over for the girls. Dollar Bill backs out of the 7-11 and drives up the street. He pulls into the parking lot of the strip club and parks. Getting out of his car, Dollar Bill approaches GOLDY and gives him dapps.

GOLDY

Dollar, what's up cool whip?

DOLLAR BILL

What's up chocolate bar?

GOLDY

I seen that fine ass little snow bunny you cracked. That bitch is hot! I ain't mad at you pimpin'.

DOLLAR BILL

And you know this man, I keep my pimp game strong. In a minute you fools gonna be callin' me Fort Knox.

GOLDY

I feel you cool whip. Hey you hear about that fool Jumbo getting burnt up? That shit just ain;'t right. But since that fool died, man I been cleaning up on the track. Nigga, I made two G's already tonight.

DOLLAR BILL

His death was fucked up. But I ain't doin' too bad myself, tonight.

Too-Tall pulls up in a Cadillac STS. and gets out joining Dollar Bill and another pimp (GOLDY) He gives them both dapps.

DOLLAR BILL

(to Too-Tall)
What's crackin' giant?

TOO-TALL

My money. What's up Dollar, what's up Goldy?

GOLDY

What's up tall man? Damn nigga, how tall is your ass?

TOO-TALL

Seven feet and long, that's all you need to know.

DOLLAR BILL

Damn Tall, we wasn't tryin' to hear all your business now.

TOO-TALL

My dick even got his own name. Too-Long -Strong.

GOLDY

Nigga we don't want to hear about your little wee-wee.

All three begin laughing together, as they watch up and down the street.

TOO-TALL

Fuck you short stuff. Don't hate cause you got the Little Man Syndrome.

Tiger drives up in a shiny white convertible Jaguar. He joins the group giving everyone dapps.

TOO-TALL

What's up T-I-G?

TIGER

What's up Tall, Dollar, Goldy? Damn Too-Tall you a tall ass nigga. Shit

Dollar Bill, Goldy, and Too-Tall all start laughing again.

TOO-TALL

Fuck you Tiger. Fuck you 'all. You all just mad cause you ain't lookin' as fine as me.

Down at the other end of Sunset Blvd., the detective in plain-clothes cruises by in an unmarked Lexus 400GS. A prostitute is walking on the other side of the street. He makes a u-turn in the middle of the street and pulls into a gas station and parks in front of the wall. He gets out and sits on the hood of the car. As the prostitute (JUMBO'S HO) walks by, the detective speaks to her.

DETECTIVE

How you doin' tonight?

JUMBO'S HO

Can I help you with something?

DETECTIVE

I hope you can, I have money.

JUMBO'S HO

What you want, a blow job, some pussy, how much money you wanna spend?

The detective whips out his badge and flashes it in her face.

DETECTIVE

What I want to do is take your ass to jail. I'm a cop.

JUMBO'S HO

> Shit! I'll do whatever you want, just don't take me to jail.

DETECTIVE

> Here's my card. I'm Detective Brown, Day Brown. I just want some answers and then you can go. So what do you know about Jumbo's murder? I know you are one of Jumbo's hos'.

JUMBO'S HO

> Look Officer Brown, I don't know anything about Jumbo's murder., I promise you.

DETECTIVE

> When was the last time you saw Jumbo?

JUMBO'S HO

> The last time I saw him was about ten on Friday night. He dropped us off for work, and that was the last time I seen him.

DETECTIVE

> Why do I think you are lying to me? Turn around and put your hands behind your back. You are under arrest for soliciting a police officer. You have the right to remain silent, you have the right to an attorney, and any thing you say can and will be held against you in a court of law. Do you understand these rights?

He grabs her roughly, handcuffing her as she struggles and curses.

JUMBO'S HO

> Get your hands off me, fuckin' pig! I wouldn't tell you shit even if I did know!

Now in handcuffs, she continues to struggle, kicking and cursing as the detective drags her into his car.

Back in the parking lot of the strip club, Dollar Bill and his group are joined by another group of pimps, (K-D & RABBIT) all drinking, talking, and some of them shooting dice. Dollar Bill rolls the dice.

DOLLAR BILL

> Seven eleven! Hit 'em girl!. My hos need a new pair a pumps. God damned jinky ass dice. Shit. Here, shoot twenty.

He throws down twenty dollars. Rabbit picks the dice up off the ground and throws them.

RABBIT

> Gimme the fuckin' dice. I'm gonna show you 'all how to shoot these bitches. Break 'em. God damned dice, I lost again. These mother fuckers must be loaded. Shit, it don't matter. My ho's already made me fifteen hundred tonight. With most of Jumbo's girls gone, I'm cleanin'up.

Tiger picks up the dice and takes his turn.

TIGER

> Gimme those dice. Stop cryin' like little girls and take lessons from an old school player. Hit 'em! Seven!!! See what I'm talkin' about young bucks, take lessons. Let me pick my god damned money up. One mo time! Hit 'em! Eleven!! I'm just too damned good. Who bet I hit?

Tiger gathers up his money. Rabbit, Dollar Bill, K-D, and Goldy all toss their money on the ground in a pile.

RABBIT

> Nigga I bet you don't hit.

DOLLAR BILL

> I'm on that bet, shit.

K-D

> Tiger, you ain't gonna hit shit.

GOLDY

> I want a piece of that pie. You ain't gonna do it three times.

K-D

> Shoot nigga, don't be "scurred". A scared man can't win.

Tiger shakes the dice throwing them confidently.

TIGER

> You fools about to lose all your shit. Buck 'em! Seven! One more time. Pay a player.

Tiger, laughing, gathers up all the money. Dollar Bill's cell phone rings. He answers.

DOLLAR BILL

> Yo. What's up baby. Where you at? . . . I'm shootin' dice . . . I'm on my way. Peace out . . . (to group) I'll see you'all niggas later.

Back on Sunset Blvd, Sunny waves at Dollar Bill. He pulls over, letting her get in and they drive off together.

SUNNY

There's so much money out here tonight. God damn. I told you baby. Here's four hundred right here.

DOLLAR BILL

You wasn't bullshitin'. Niggas getting' paid tonight Bitch, give my money.

SUNNY

So did you win shootin' dice? Dollar look! See that pimp in the Corvette? That's K-D.

DOLLAR BILL

I was just shootin' dice with that nigga. I heard he got it goin' on.

SUNNY

He got about ten girls on the track, takin' your money Dollar. We take him outa the box, another step up! He always sweatin' me.

DOLLAR BILL

Fuck it. Another nigga gonna bite the dust, let's do it.

Dollar Bill and Sunny spot Indio getting into another car. They follow the car around the corner to an alley. where it stops and parks. Dollar Bill, turning off his headlights, pulls over and parks further down the street. Turning to Sunny.

DOLLAR BILL

Listen, this is how we gonna get K-D's ass . . .

Inside the tricks car, Indio and the trick (TRICK 5) are arguing.

TRICK 5

Why we just can't go to my house?

INDIO

You cute and all but I gotta make my money. I can't go to your house. So what you wanna' do cause I ain't goin;' to your house.

TRICK 5

You just like the rest of those bitches. I thought you was different.

INDIO

Baby why you trippin' I ain't your bitch.

Indio jumps out of the car and walks out of the alley. The trick jumps out after her and grabs her arm. Dollar Bill seeing the commotion jumps out of his car with a 14" pipe in his hand. Running toward Indio, he cracks the trick across the head with one clean stroke. The trick falls to the ground unconscious.

DOLLAR BILL

You all right? How much money he give you?

INDIO

I'm alright. Here's sixty dollars.

DOLLAR BILL

Put the sixty dollars back in his pocket so he can't say you robbed him. And let's ride.

Indio and Dollar Bill run to the car. Sunny pulls up in the drivers seat, motor running, throws open the door, and they both dive in as Sunny takes off.

INDIO

I wanted to laugh so bad when you cracked that trick over the head. My hero.

DOLLAR BILL

I'm just doing what an investor gets paid to do.

Back inside the condo, Indio is in the kitchen cooking, Sunny is sitting on the couch watching T.V. and Dollar Bill is in the master bedroom kneeling in front of the open safe, counting money. Sunny gets up off the couch and joins Dollar Bill in the master bedroom.

SUNNY

How much do we have?

DOLLAR BILL

We made five grand this week, counting the dope money. We about to take over this mothea fuckin'.

SUNNY

I know baby. And I promise I won't let you down. You got two bad bitches on your team, now.

INDIO

Come and get it! Dinners ready!

SUNNY

Coming! But I gotta shower first!

INDIO

Ok! Dollar, want your plate now?!

DOLLAR BILL

Yeah!

Sunny strips naked, stepping out of her clothes as she walks into the shower. Dollar Bill smiling, admiring her ass as she walks by him, still kneeling in front of the safe with the money in his hand. Placing the money inside the safe, and closing the door, he heads toward the kitchen where Indio greets him with a full plate of food, steak, eggs, hash browns, Caesar salad, and toast.

INDIO

Here Dollar, I hope you like it. I love to cook!

DOLLAR BILL

Damn girl, you outdid yourself this time. This sho' look good!

INDIO

Sit down baby and let me get you something to drink.

Dollar Bill, taking his plate, walks over to the couch and sits down, placing his food on the coffee table, he begins eating.

INDIO

What do you want to drink? Soda, wine, juice?

DOLLAR BILL

Gimme some red Kool-Aid.

Indio walks into the living room, carrying a plate of food and a glass of red Kool-Aid. She hands the glass to Dollar Bill, then sits down beside him and begins eating. Sunny walks into the living room wearing a see-through silk robe

INDIO

I made your plate girl, want me to get it for you?

SUNNY

I'm cool girl. I'll get it.

DOLLAR BILL

This shit good than a motha fucka.

INDIO

So Dollar, what's gonna happen to all of Jumbo's girls.

Sunny returns to the living room with a plate of food and sits down between Dollar Bill and Indio on the couch.

SUNNY

Either they got to choose another pimp or leave the track.

DOLLAR BILL

Most of them hos' are so scared by his murder they already left the track.

SUNNY

Let me scoot my big butt in here some more.

INDIO

Girl your butt ain't big, it's something to hold on to.

Indio makes humping gestures with her hips. They all laugh together.

INDIO

Bang, bang, bang, bang!

DOLLAR BILL

Girl, you so stupid with your crazy ass. jokes.

The news is heard on the T.V talking about Jumbo's murder.

SUNNY

I wonder if one of his hos did it.

INDIO

> Girl, I hear he be beatin' his hos' bad with the pimp stick. Maybe they got tired of the pimp stick and killed his ass.

DOLLAR BILL

> Can you two change the conversation? Let the man rest in peace. Him and his pimp stick.

Next afternoon, the sun is shining through the window, the T.V. is still on. Dollar Bill, Indio and Sunny are still on the couch sprawled out on top of each other, empty plates and cups are on the coffee table. Dollar Bill's cell phone rings. He wakes up and answers the phone, rubbing his eyes.

DOLLAR BILL

> Yo.

TIGER

> Get your white boy ass up. It's one o'clock in the afternoon.

DOLLAR BILL

> Are you serious?

TIGER

> Do hos' sell pussy?

DOLLAR BILL

> Not all of 'em.

TIGER

> Listen sleeping beauty, I got one of my guys comin' in with some heaters, you wanna cop one of 'em? After that shit happen with Jumbo, I ain't goin' out like no sucker, you feel me?

DOLLAR BILL

Hell yea I want one. What he got?

TIGER

Nigga, he got those sixteen shot glocks.

DOLLAR BILL

What's the goin' rate?

TIGER

Three-fifty still in the box, clean, no dirt, with a box of shells. You in or out?

DOLLAR BILL

I'm in, T baby. Get it for me and I'll give you the money later on tonight.

TIGER

That's official, white boy. I'll peep you later on the track. Peace out.

The girls begin stretching and rubbing their eyes as they wake up.

SUNNY

Who was you talkin' to Dollar?

DOLLAR BILL

Tiger.

SUNNY

What did Tiger want this early in the morning?

DOLLAR BILL

Early in the morning my ass. It's after one o'clock in the afternoon.

INDIO

> For real? Damn. It sure feel good to sleep in for a change.

Dollar Bill dials the phone.

DOLLAR BILL

> Yo, Tiger, Can I meet you in about an hour and bring you the money?

TIGER

> You can do that. I just had him on the phone. I'll have 'em by the time you get here.

DOLLAR BILL

> Meet me in the back of the parking lot of the record store, the one across the street from Jack in the box. I'll be there at two. Is that cool?

TIGER

> I'm there.

Dollar Bill hangs up the phone. He walks into one of the other rooms to the closet and pulls out baggy jeans, a T-shirt, Nike tennis shoes, and a baseball cap with the letters "COMPTON". Returning to the living room he sets the clothes down and strips naked.

INDIO

> Damn dollar, Can I have some dick? Bang, bang, bang, bang

All three begin laughing as Dollar Bill finishes dressing.

DOLLAR BILL

> No, you can't have no dick. So bang on this.

He holds up his middle finger.

SUNNY

He do have some good dick, girl!.

INDIO

I know he do girl, and there's a lot of bad dick out there!

SUNNY

Amen to that.

Dollar Bill, now dressed, heads to the front door.

DOLLAR BILL

I'm about to make moves so I'll see you two later.

SUNNY

Love you baby, be careful.

INDIO

Bye-bye good dick.

DOLLAR BILL

Unbelievable. Call me if you go anywhere.

He walks out closing the door behind him.

INDIO

How we gonna go anywhere, Dollar got the car.?

SUNNY

We have two cars.

INDIO

> Damn, he has two cars? Most pimps don't have two cars. Some pimps don't even have one car. And he let you drive one by yourself?

SUNNY

> Girl, I do what ever I wannna do. You gotta understand. You are dealin' with a real man now, not a tennis shoe pimp.

INDIO

> Tennis shoe pimps, they ain't nothin' but haters. If only all their hos' knew what it feels like to be with a real pimp, all them hos be choosin' a real pimp, like Dollar Bill. And tennis shoe pimps wouldn't be pimpin' no more.

In the parking lot behind the record store. Dollar and Tiger are standing outside their cars talking. Tiger opens his trunk.

DOLLAR BILL

> Let me see what you got for me?

TIGER

> Peep these mother fuckers out, playboy. These bitches are sweet.

DOLLAR BILL

> Now that's beautiful.

TIGER

> What I tell you white boy.

DOLLAR BILL

> Tiger, you the man, baby, you be comin' through for a brother.

Reaching into his pocket, he pulls out some bills in a gold money clip and hands it to Tiger. Reaching into the trunk he lifts out the gun and stuffs it inside his waistband.

TIGER

Don't forget to take your shells, bud.

DOLLAR BILL

Good lookin' baby

TIGER

You on the track tonight?

DOLLAR BILL

Always. My hos made crazy loot last night.

TIGER

So did mine. Nigga, and I took all those fools money in the dice game last night. I'm thinkin' about takin' my hos on a vacation to the Carribean next month.

DOLLAR BILL

How much you hit 'em for?

TIGER

Fifteen hundred dollars, nigga.

DOLLAR BILL

God damn nigga, I know those fools was pissed off.

TIGER

I told them young bucks about fucking with this old school nigga. I do this shit for a living, hear?

DOLLAR BILL

Once again, you the man.

TIGER

> I gotta get home to my wife, I'm married. I can't be out here bull shittin' with you. Some of us got responsibilities.

DOLLAR BILL

> Yea right. Get the fuck outa here with that bullshit.

DOLLAR BILL

> Peace out cracker. See ya on the track.

TIGER

> You just mad cause I'm white and pretty nigga. I can't say that about your ugly black ass.

Pulling into the driveway of Dollar Bill's mothers house in Compton. Dollar bill parks, gets out of the car and walks through the unlocked door. He walks through the living room into the kitchen and opens the refrigerator, He grabs a pitcher of red Kool-Aid and drinks from it before putting it back inside.

DOLLAR BILL

> Mom! Mom, you here!

Dollar Bill's mother enters the living room from the hallway.

MOM

> I'm here Shawn, where you at?

DOLLAR BILL

> I'm in the kitchen.

Dollar bill walks back into the living room and gives his mother a hug.

MOM

      Where the hell you been boy?

Mom walks over to a table in the living room where a jig saw puzzle is half completed. She sits down and begins working on the puzzle.

DOLLAR BILL

      Just takin' care of business, gettin' my loot.

MOM

      You not out there sellin' dope again are you?

Dollar Bill hands his mom a large roll of money wrapped up in rubber bands.

DOLLAR BILL

      No, I have a job.

MOM

      Thank you for the money Shawn. I could sure use some right now. And what job you got?

DOLLAR BILL

      I'm an investor.

MOM

      Don't be lyin' to me boy or I'll knock you down.

DOLLAR BILL

      No shit, I ain't lyin' I gotta roll now little dog, I got appointments. Peace out woman, I love you.

MOM

      I love you to. Be careful, whatever it is you doin'.

Dollar Bill, now back inside his car pulls out of the driveway, as he talks on his cell phone.

SUNNY

We been worried crazy about you. We been callin' and callin' and callin' When you didn't answer the phone, we thought something was wrong.

DOLLAR BILL

I apologize for that. I' went to my mom's house and the phone was in the car so I didn't hear it ring.

INDIO

Is he alright, he ok, let me talk to his ass.

SUNNY

Here's Indio. She wants to talk to you.

INDIO

You had us scared over here. We just glad you ok.

DOLLAR BILL

The freeways backed up so be ready for work when I get there.

Dollar Bill enters through the front door of the condo and calls out playfully.

DOLLAR BILL

Lucy, I'm home!

Sunny enters the living room from the bedroom. She is dressed for work, wearing a designer blue jean dress with clear stripper shoes. She gives Dollar bill a hug and a kiss.

SUNNY

Hi Ricky. How was your day?

DOLLAR BILL

Great! You ready to do that tonight.

SUNNY

Do what?

DOLLAR BILL

K-D.

SUNNY

Ready ain't the word for it. I'm there.

Indio enters the living room wearing a black lace mini dress with black stripper shoes.

INDIO

Hi Dollar, I'm ready to go.

SUNNY

I'm ready too, whenever you are Dollar.

DOLLAR BILL

Good. Bout time you hos' be ready on time. Now you can wait for me for a change and watch me prance around in front of the mirror trying on different outfits. "How do I look, how do I look, does my butt look big?"

Both girls laugh at Dollar Bill.

SUNNY

Shut up and get dressed, big head.

Dollar Bill, Sunny and Indio are inside the car parked on the side of Sunset Blvd. Indio jumps out and the car pulls back into traffic.

DOLLAR BILL

> Try to get K-D to pull over for you.

SUNNY

> Shit, that's the easy part.

DOLLAR BILL

> And if you can, have him get a room, and if not we go to plan B.

SUNNY

> I'll have his head between my legs so fast. Dollar! There he is now, in that red corvette. Let me out, let me out.

Dollar Bill speeds up driving by K-D who is talking to a prostitute. Dollar Bill pulls over and stops, Sunny jumps out and walks back towards K-D. Dollar Bill continues down the street, making a u-turn at the next light, seeing K-D who is now talking to Sunny, he pulls over and parks.

K-D

> Say ho, when you gonna choose a real player with real money.

SUNNY

> I have a real player.

K-D

> Bitch, you don't have shit but a punk ass white boy.

K-D jumps out of his car and grabs Sunny roughly by her arm.

SUNNY

You better get your motha fuckin' hands off me nigga!

K-D

Shut the fuck up ho, I'm about to break your ass now bitch.

SUNNY

Ok, ok. I'm sorry K-D. Please don't tell Dollar.

K-D

Didn't I tell you to shut the fuck up, ho? Do what the fuck you told! Bitch, give me your purse . . . Forty dollars! That's all you got?

SUNNY

I'm sorry, I'm sorry! That's all I got. Please don't tell Dollar! Just get a room so we can kick it.

K-D

Bitch, don't fuck with me or I'll kill your ass ho.

SUNNY

I ain't fuckin' with you. I'm ready to choose anyway.

K-D

Get the fuck in the car, bitch.

He pushes Sunny into the car. K-D struts proudly to the drivers side and gets in. He drives off and Dollar Bill follows them from a distance. K-D pulls up to his motel and parks.

K-D

Let's go bitch. I got a room already.

SUNNY

> You live here?

K-D

> Bitch, you think K-D would live in a shit hole like this? My hos' work out of this room. Get your ass out and open my door for me, bitch.

Sunny obediently jumps out of the Corvette, hurrying around to the drivers side and opens the door. K-D gets out, grabbing Sunny by the arm again, dragging her up the stairs. He unlocks the door with the other hand, and shoves her inside the opened door. He locks the door carefully behind him.

K-D

> Bitch, get naked and let me see what you working with.

Sunny glances nervously at the locked door. She looks around, seeing a CD player, she walks over and pushes the play button and turns up the volume. She begins to dance provocatively as she is stripping until naked except for her shoes.

SUNNY

> Can I use the rest room, I gotta pee.

K-D

> I told you don't be fucking with me ho. Hurry up bitch.

Sonny, walks into the bathroom, locking the door behind her and begins pacing nervously. She notices a mirror on the sink. She picks up the mirror, flushes the toilet, and throws the mirror on the floor. The mirror shatters making a loud noise. She immediately unlocks the door as K-D rushes in.

K-D

Bitch what the fuck you doin in here?

SUNNY

I'm sorry daddy. It was an accident. I was fixin' my hair for you and the mirror fell off the sink.

Sunny ran out of the bathroom, leaving him standing there. Looking over her shoulder, she unlocks the front door, then leaps onto the bed and spreads her legs. K-D hurries in behind her.

K-D

Now that's what the fuck I'm talking about.

SUNNY

I've been wantin' to fuck you for a long time.

K-D strips naked and climbs on top of Sunny and begins fucking her. Dollar bursts into the room carrying a baseball bat, and kicks the door shut behind him. K-D, startled, freezes and looks at Dollar Bill.

K-D

What the fuck is this shit!

Dollar Bill slams the bat over K-D's head over and over and over.

DOLLAR BILL

You son of a bitch. You think you was gonna fuck my girl without payin', mother fucker. This ain't Burger King "have it your way" bitch.

SUNNY

Dollar! Dollar, stop, stop, Dollar stop!

K-D's body collapses on Sunny. Dollar Bill, breathing heavily finally stops, wiping the bat with the corner of a sheet, he tosses it on K-D's body. Sunny wiggles out from under the lifeless K-D. She runs into the bathroom, using a towel to turn on the water, she jumps in the shower, still wearing her shoes, and washes herself off. Dollar Bill is watching out the window. Sunny, dripping wet, runs back into the room, drying off with a towel. Dollar Bill points at the table.

DOLLAR BILL

> Take that towel and wipe off every thing you touched. And hurry up.

SUNNY

> Dollar, I picked up the mirror and broke it, its still on the floor.

DOLLAR BILL

> Use that towel, wet it in the toilet, and sweep up the floor with it. Get every last piece of glass. That way we take the fingerprints with us.

Sunny quickly follows Dollar Bill's directions as he continues watching out the window. Sunny throws on her dress and picks up the glass wrapped up in the towel. They walk calmly out the door and down the stairs. They walk around behind the motel to an alley where Dollar Bill's car is parked. He pops the trunk and pulls out a trash bag. Sunny sets down the towel with the glass inside, they both take off their shoes and drop them in the trash bag. Sunny reaches in the trunk and pulls out clean shoes for both of them as Dollar Bill throws the trash bag back in the trunk. Rapidly pulling on their clean shoes, Sunny then picks up the towels. Dollar Bill slams the trunk shut and they hurry back inside the car. They calmly drive off turning down a deserted side street.

DOLLAR BILL

> When I tell you to, I want you to hold the towel out the window, letting the glass sprinkle on the ground

as I drive. Then I'll let you know when to drop the
towel.

SUNNY

We lucky baby. The plan almost got fucked up when
he locked the door on me. I had to think for a minute,
and all I kept hearing in my head was your voice
saying to me, always have a back up, always have a
back up, and this mirror, unexpectedly, became my
back up. Next time let's have a better plan

DOLLAR BILL

Bitch what? Next time! What the fuck you mean next
time. Ok now, dump the glass out like I told ya and
be careful so nothin' falls back inside.

SUNNY

Ok baby

DOLLAR BILL

I'm gonna drop you back off on the track and check
on Indio. Now drop the towel.

Back on Sunset Blvd. Dollar Bill pulls over, Sunny jumps out of the
car and he pulls off. Up ahead he can see Indio climbing into another
car. He follows the car to an alley where it parks. He parks up the street
watching and waiting . . . Forty minutes later, looking at his watch . . .

DOLLAR BILL

Forty fucking minutes again. Unbelievable.

Dollar Bill gets out of his car and walks up to the tricks car and
opens the passenger door. Indio is riding the trick (TRICK-6) in the
passenger seat aggressively. they both looked at Dollar bill shocked.

DOLLAR BILL

> Bitch, get the fuck out of the car now! What the fuck takin' you so god damned long.?

INDIO

> I'm tryin' to get my nut off, hold on baby, I'm about to come, I'm about to come right now.

DOLLAR BILL

> Ho bring your ass on and get the fuck outa this car. Now!

Indio jumps off the trick and out of the car pulling up her panties. Angry but amused, Dollar Bill shakes his head in disbelief. Walking away, he begins mocking her.

DOLLAR BILL

> "I'm trying to get my nut off" Crazy fuckin' ho! Unbelievable.

INDIO

> Wait Dollar!

DOLLAR BILL

> Bitch you in there fucking that mother fuckin' trick like you payin' him.

INDIO

> I'm sorry Dollar, it won't happen again.

Indio, sheepishly follows Dollar Bill back to his car and they both get in. Dollar Bill looks over at Indio angrily, then bursts out laughing. as they drive off.

INDIO

> What are you laughin' about? You not mad?

DOLLAR BILL

Bitch I'm mad as fuck. But that shit was funny though, "I'm tryin' to get mine, I'm about to come". Ho, I ain't never heard no shit like that before! Where's my money?

INDIO

Here's two hundred and fifty dollars. You sure you not mad?

DOLLAR BILL

What the fuck was you thinkin'?

INDIO

He was about to make me come Dollar. You know that feelin' when you just right there and you gotta get it.

DOLLAR BILL

Bitch, you fuckin him like he was your man. He ain't your boyfriend. He's a mother fuckin' trick. Get the fuck out, I'm gonna go check on Sunny.

Dollar Bill pulls over and Indio jumps out of the car, walking towards Sunset Blvd. as the car pulls off.

Dollar Bill, now driving back on Sunset Blvd. pulls over to pick up Sunny. Sunny gets in the car and they drive off.

DOLLAR BILL

How you feelin' you ok?

SUNNY

Hell yea, I'm cool, fuck K-D, bitch ass nigga. Here, I made two hundred dollars while you was gone

DOLLAR BILL

Are you ok to go back to work.

SUNNY

Yep, let me out right here.

Dollar Bill pulls over, Sunny puts the money in the glove box and gets out of the car. As Dollar Bill drives off. the cell phone rings and he answers it.

DOLLAR BILL

Yo.

HOSTESS

Hi Dollar Bill, it's me!

DOLLAR BILL

Who's me?

HOSTESS-MYA

It's me, Mya, your waitress from Dennys. You offered me a job.

DOLLAR BILL

Ok, ok. I remember. So how you doin' Mya.

MYA

I've been thinking about what you said and I'm tired of working for chump change. I'm about to move out of my roommates house.

DOLLAR BILL

So, are you callin' me for a place to stay or you ready to choose?

MYA

I'm ready to have my money invested, so can you pick me up.

DOLLAR BILL

Where you at?

About thirty minutes later, Dollar Bill pulls over where Mya, dressed in a flowered summer dress, is standing on the curb with a large duffle bag at her side. She picks up her bag, throws it in the back seat, and happily bounces into the front seat and they drive off.

MYA

Hi Dollar Bill. Thank you for picking me up.

DOLLAR BILL

No, thank you. It's a privilege to pick you up. you have any money on you?

MYA

I have a hundred dollars in my purse. You want it?

DOLLAR BILL

Yes, that would be nice.

Mya reaches in her purse, pulling out a hundred dollar bill, and hands it over to Dollar Bill. He takes her money and puts it in his pocket.

DOLLAR BILL

Thank you. Have you ever sold pussy before?

MYA

No, but I can learn. I've been told I have some good pussy. I've never had a one night stand yet, cause they always come back for more.

DOLLAR BILL

You got any stripper shoes in that bag?

MYA

Yes. Should I put them on now?

DOLLAR BAG

Most definitely.

Mya leans over the back seat, exposing her ass. Dollar bill glances over and smiles at the view. She opens her bag and pulls out stripper shoes and puts them on.

DOLLAR BILL

Are you ready to turn your first trick.

MYA

I guess so.

DOLLAR BILL

Well let's make history then.

Now, back on Sunset Blvd. They are driving around as Dollar Bill points out their spots in the alleys. She listens quietly while he schools her. Finally Dollar Bill pulls over and parks on a side street.

MYA

Thanks for the education. I guess I'm ready.

DOLLAR BILL

Open the glove box and grab forty dollars and some condoms.

MYA

What's the forty dollars for?

DOLLAR BILL

It's for emergencies and so you can't get arrested for loitering by the police. Take your I.D.

MYA

I think I'm gonna like this job.

DOLLAR BILL

Enough talk, ho. Get the fuck out and go get my trap money.

Mya jumps out of the shiny BMW. Dollar Bill pulls off back to Sunset Blvd. Seeing Indio, he pulls over to let her in the car, and they drive off.

DOLLAR BILL

Where's Sunny at?

INDIO

She just got herself another date. There's so much money to be made out here tonight.

DOLLAR BILL

You know what I'm gonna start callin' you Indio?

INDIO

What?

DOLLAR BILL

The "I'm about to come" ho, "let me get my nut" ho. "Oooh the trick is makin' me come" ho. Wait, Dollar, wait!

INDIO

Very funny Dollar. Here's two hundred dollars.

DOLLAR BILL

>Put it in the glove box. You so funny Indio.

Dollar Bill is driving around checking their spots in the alleys. Seeing a car in one alley, Dollar Bill pulls over and parks, watching. Through the window is the outline of two people having sex.

INDIO

>Wanna hear a joke Dollar?

DOLLAR BILL

>Yea, let me hear it.

INDIO

>What do you call a ho with no panties on?

DOLLAR BILL

>What do you call a ho with no panties on? Hmmm? A ho getting' fucked?

INDIO

>Nope, you call her, a ho with no panties on.

DOLLAR BILL

>Girl I don't know what I'm gonna do with your crazy ass. Unbelievable.

Mya gets out of the parked car, Dollar bill flashes the lights, and she walks over to the car and jumps in as they all drive off.

MYA

>Here Dollar, I got fifty dollars out of him.

DOLLAR BILL

>Hand it over. Mya, you remember Indio. Indio this is Mya from the Dennys.

INDIO

What's up girlfriend. Welcome to the family. Damn dollar you hooked this one up.

MYA

Hi Indio.

INDIO

Hey girl. I knew you was gonna call.

MYA

How'd you know that?

INDIO

When you took the number and didn't give it back. That's when you know a ho is ready. And feel free to say what's on your mind to Dollar, he don't care.

DOLLAR BILL

You just put my shit in the street butt naked ready to be run over.

INDIO

There go Sunny right there.

Dollar Bill making a U-turn in the middle of the street, pulls over and Sunny jumps in. They all drive off.

MYA

Hey girl. I'm Mya. Remember me.

SUNNY

Hey, what's up girl. Good to see you again. You look so different without your uniform on. You sexy girl! Welcome to the family!

MYA

I feel like family already.

SUNNY

You are family. You at home now, girl. Dollar I'm so hungry baby. Can't we go eat now?

INDIO

Sunny what happened to the new stripper shoes you had on earlier?

SUNNY

The heel broke off those motha fuckas.

Back at the condo, Dollar Bill and all three girls walk through the front door. Dollar Bill collapses on the couch, along with Indio and Sunny. Mya walks around the room, looking around.

MYA

Wow! This is soo beautiful! Whose house is this?

INDIO

I said the same thing the first time I walked in here. It's your house now.

DOLLAR BILL

So does it have your approval? Do you like it? Or you think we should move?

MYA

Do I like it? I'll die here. I love it.

DOLLAR BILL

There's four bedrooms. Sleep anywhere you want, this is your home now. Don't ask, do what you want around here.

MYA

Where is your room Indio?

INDIO

I don't have my own room, I sleep with Dollar Bill and Sunny. Sunny and I are both bi. I know you're not into girls and that's cool.

MYA

You don't care that I'm not bisexual?

SUNNY

No, we don't care. We family, we don't trip like that. Just be yourself.

MYA

I'll take a bedroom next to you guys so I can still be close to everybody.

SUNNY

That' so sweet girl. Come here and give me a hug.

Mya walks over to Sunny and embraces her.

MYA

That feels so good girl. No one has hugged me like that since my mom died.

Indio heads to the kitchen and begins cooking. Dollar Bill gets up and walks into the master bedroom opening the safe, and Sunny follows behind him. He begins counting money. As Sunny sits on the bed. Maya walks off toward another room.

SUNNY

How much money do we have?

DOLLAR BILL

Almost two hundred thousand. One day we gonna all retire.

SUNNY

One day I'm gonna buy me a big ass house with a swimming pool with that money.

DOLLAR BILL

Why the fuck you always talkin' about what you gonna buy. Its always me, me, me, me, me, me. It's never us. It's all about you, yourself and yours. Sometimes I feel like you be settin' me up girl.

SUNNY

Fuck you! You know what I mean!. Don't you ever talk to me like that, sayin' I'm tryin' to set you up.

DOLLAR BILL

Bitch. You just remember who run this shit here. You don't run shit but your motha fuckin' mouth. Cause bitch I don't need your ass. I'll give you half this fuckin' money and you can get the fuck up outa here right now!

SUNNY

You right Dollar, I'm sorry, I'm trippin'.

INDIO

Dollar! Sunny! Hurry! Look, come'ere you guys!!

Dollar Bill, Sunny and Mya all rush back into the living room where Indio is standing in front of the T.V.

DOLLAR BILL

What's up, girl?

INDIO

They found another pimp beat to death in his motel room tonight.

They all plop down on the couch staring at the T.V. set.

SUNNY

Damn dollar, you better watch yourself. There's a serial pimp killer running around out there.

DOLLAR BILL

Don't worry. I got some fire for his ass.

INDIO

Are you guys still hungry?

DOLLAR BILL

No, I lost my appetite. Thanks anyway Indio.

SUNNY

I was hungry, but after watchin' this shit on T.V. I lost my appetite too. I'm worried about somethin' happenin' to Dollar.

INDIO

I hear you girl.

MYA

Wow! That's scary. But I'm still hungry!

Next morning, in Mya's bedroom, Mya climbs out of her bed and walks into the living room. Dollar Bill is asleep on the couch. Mya gently shakes him and he awakens.

MYA

Dollar, Dollar.

DOLLAR BILL

What's up Mya.

MYA

Can you and Sunny take me to pick up the rest of my things?

DOLLAR BILL

Go wake up Sunny. We'll take you.

Mya enters the bedroom where Sunny and Indio are cuddled up asleep on the bed. Mya shakes Sunny to wake her.

SUNNY

Hey girl, you ok?

MYA

Can you and Dollar take me to pick up the rest of my things? I asked Dollar and he said ok, to ask you first.

SUNNY

Just let me get dressed first.

Inside the police station the detective is yelling at everyone. All around are policeman bringing in prostitutes, thugs, guys dressed as girls, and homeless bums, all in handcuffs passing by for processing. Other policemen are sitting at their desks writing or talking on the phone. A policeman passes by the detective with a sheep on a leash.

DETECTIVE

What the fuck is going on around here? We have two dead pimps, no witnesses, no leads, no suspects, can anyone please tell me what the fuck is going on around here! Why do we have nothing??!!!

OFFICER 2

> Detective, take a look at this. This file just came in.
> The guy who was killed last night, his name is Kenny
> Dunn, a.k.a. K-D. He was arrested two months ago
> on a terrorist threat to kill Jumbo over a dispute
> about money. One of K-D's girls informed us that
> Jumbo owed K-D money over a drug deal gone bad.
> And here's where it gets real good. One of Jumbo's
> girls attempted to kill K-D coming out of a strip club
> two weeks prior to his murder. The next day the girls
> body was found in an alley beat to death.

DETECTIVE

> What the hell is goin' on here. We are missing
> something and it's right in our face. I want every
> officer in the briefing room in fifteen minutes!

Back inside the condo in the living room everyone is awake. Dollar Bill,
Mya, and Indio are on the couch, Sunny is walking out of the bedroom.

DOLLAR BILL

> Let's roll. Indio, you coming or you staying home?

INDIO

> I'm stayin' home to work on my tan by the pool.

DOLLAR BILL

> We up outa here then. See ya later.

In the police briefing room, the room is filled with officers sitting and
standing. The detective is at the front of the room addressing everyone.

DETECTIVE

> Ok now people. Listen up. We have a killer, or killers
> on our hands and we don't know a god damned
> thing. I want every officer on the street tonight, if

anything even looks out of place, you better be on it like stink on shit. Now everybody get the fuck outa here and go find me a killer.

Outside of an apartment complex, Sunny and Dollar Bill are sitting in the car talking.

SUNNY

Sorry about last night Dollar. SCOOBY should be the next one to go.

DOLLAR BILL

You know what, I was thinkin' the same shit. He got too many hos on the track and too many big connections. But this is gonna be the last one. Remember, rule number three; never get greedy.

SUNNY

You know what I heard from one of his hos' last night.

DOLLAR BILL

What's that?

SUNNY

You know Tuesday and Thursdays are vice night, right. I heard he pays off the cops not to arrest his girls on Tuesday and Thursdays. His girls are the only ones that never go to jail on vice night.

DOLLAR BILL

You know what, I heard that rumor too. But we got one problem. Scooby is flying to Miami tonight.

SUNNY

Oh shit.

DOLLAR

Fuck it we just gonna do two in a row. We take him outa the box tonight.

Back inside the condo Maya is in her bedroom unpacking and Indio is standing in front of the refrigerator. Dollar Bill is in front of the safe and Sunny is standing next to him.

SUNNY

I love you.

DOLLAR BILL

Get ready. We goin' shopping, let's throw a little money around.

SUNNY

We are? Let me go tell the girls.

Maya is walking into the kitchen as Sunny rushes in.

SUNNY

We're goin' shoppin' right now, so get ready!

MYA

We are?!

INDIO

Hell yea, that's what I'm talkin' about.

At the mall, inside Bloomingdales they make an entrance walking in all together arm and arm like they own the place. Then the girls begin running around gleefully in and out of the dressing room, dressing and undressing, modeling for each other. The salesclerks running around after them trying to keep up. In another department in the dressing room, Dollar Bill is trying on suits with the help of a SALESPERSON. Dollar Bill heads out.

SALESPERSON

You can't walk out with the suit on.! It's against store policy!

DOLLAR BILL

Don't worry, I can afford this shit.

SALESPERSON

I'm gonna call security.

Dollar Bill reaches in the pocket of the suit and pulls out a fist-sized roll of bills and hands it to the salesperson.

DOLLAR BILL

Here, hold this. Still wanna call security?

SALESPERSON

I, I, I, I totally apologize to you sir. Thank you for shopping at Bloomingdales. Need anything, just ask for Stan.

Dollar bill walks through the store with the tags on his new suit and joins the girls.

INDIO

Damn, look at Dollar. Damn baby you look good.

DOLLAR BILL

So what' s the verdict?

MYA

Oooh Dollar. You gotta get that suit, you look too good in it with your fine ass.

SUNNY

That is nice. It wouldn't be right if he didn't buy that suit.

DOLLAR BILL

See anything you guys like?

INDIO

You see that cash register over there with all those clothes on it. We like everything.

DOLLAR BILL

Here, see if this will cover it. It's about four thousand. If you need more just holler.

Dollar Bill, Sunny, Indio and Mya walk out of Bloomingdales, loaded down with bags, smiling and laughing.

Later that night, they are all in the car driving down Sunset Blvd, where other prostitutes are already out on the street.

DOLLAR BILL

There's a lot of traffic tonight. Money lookin' real good.

INDIO

Every night is a good night for me, shit.

Dollar Bill pulls over, Mya and Indio get out, and he pulls off.

DOLLAR BILL

You ready?

SUNNY

Yep. I'm ready. What's wrong?

DOLLAR BILL

> What's wrong? I don't feel like you here with me right now. You sure you ready to do this shit tonight. Cause if not, you let me know now.

SUNNY

> I'm fine. Dollar stop trippin' on me, alright? Let me out right here.

Dollar Bill pulls over and Sunny jumps out without looking back. Dollar Bill pulls off and pulls into the strip club parking lot. He parks, gets out, and walks up to Goldy, giving him dapps.

DOLLAR BILL

> What's up, Playboy. Vice all over the place tonight.

GOLDY

> What's up cool whip? That's fucked up what happened to K-D last night. That's why vice is all over the place. Fuckin' pigs.

DOLLAR BILL

> You ain't lyin' man, it is fucked up.

GOLDY

> I don't give a fuck about vice, I know a bitch better have my money. or I'm gonna put the smack down on her ass. Fuckin' hos'.

DOLLAR BILL

> You a wild boy Goldy."

Another pimp pulls into the parking lot driving a silver convertible Mercedes Benz with the top down. The pimp (SCOOBY) is sitting in his car and talking on his cell phone. Dollar Bill approaches.

DOLLAR BILL

Scooby Dooby Doooo.

SCOOBY

Hold on ho . . . (to Dollar) My man Dollar, What's crackin' baby?

DOLLAR BILL

I need to holla at you later, is that cool?

SCOOBY

Hell yea that's cool my nigga. You smoke bud, don't you Dollar?

DOLLAR BILL

Blazin' them like forest fires.

SCOOBY

Meet me back here in twenty minutes, I'm gonna check on one of my hos and pick up some bud at my house.' (to ho) Bitch I'll fuck you up!

Dollar gets back in his car and races back up the street. Looking around, he spots Sunny standing by a pay phone and pulls over.

DOLLAR BILL

Get in now!

SUNNY

For what?

DOLLAR BILL

Change of plans. We gonna follow Scooby home and do his ass their.

SUNNY

> Why we changing plans now Dollar? I have a regular comin' with three hundred dollars!

DOLLAR BILL

> Fuck that! We only got twenty minutes. Bitch get your ass in the fuckin' car.

SUNNY

> Dollar, come back in five minutes. If he ain't here we're out.

Dollar Bill takes off. Sunny picks up the pay phone and dials 911.

911

> 911. Is this an emergency? How can I help you?

SUNNY

> Yes. A pimp named Scooby is gonna be murdered tonight at his house by another pimp named Shawn Watson, known as Dollar Bill.

Sunny hangs up the pay phone and carefully wipes it off with her dress while looking around. Dollar Bill pulls up just as she finishes.

DOLLAR BILL

> You ready?

SUNNY

> You gonna have to do this one by yourself. My trick is gonna pay me a thousand dollars to get another girl right now. He went to get a room and he'll be right back.

DOLLAR BILL

> Ok, I got this one. Love you.

SUNNY

     I know.

Dollar Bill pulls off making a u-turn in the middle of the street. He spots Scooby pulling out of the parking lot and follows slowly behind him. at a distance. Driving across town, Scooby finally pulls into an apartment complex. Dollar Bill watches as Scooby turns a corner out of sight then he pulls into a parking stall. Dollar Bill, looking around him, creeps out with a gun in his hand. moving quickly towards where Scooby's car turned. Scooby is now walking away from his car. He sees Dollar Bill turning the corner with the gun in his hand, as Dollar Bill aims and fires.

DOLLAR BILL

     Die Bitch!!

Dollar Bill shoots Scooby seven times. Scooby drops to the ground, choking up blood and staring at Dollar bill in disbelief. Dollar Bill runs back around the corner and jumps in his car. Before he can pull out he is suddenly surrounded by police cars, and unmarked cars. Police jump out from all sides, with their guns drawn. Dollar Bill is completely surrounded.

POLICE OFFICERS

     FREEZE! Throw your weapon out of the vehicle now!

Dollar Bill slowly throws the gun out the window.

POLICE OFFICERS

     Open the door with your right hand. Now step out of the vehicle with your hands in the air.

Dollar Bill, robot-like, exits the vehicle, with his hands in the air.

POLICE OFFICERS

> Step away from the vehicle! Lay face down on the ground with your hands behind your back! Do it now!

Dollar Bill walks backwards away from his car. and lays down on the ground putting his hands behind his back.

A week later. Dollar Bill is in prison, in prison now talking on the phone.

SUNNY

> We gonna get you outa there, baby, don't worry.

DOLLAR BILL

> I don't know what went wrong but I'm glad you wasn't there.

SUNNY

> I love you so much baby.

DOLLAR BILL

> Stop crying, I'll be alright. You just stay strong and hold down the fort while I'm gone.

SUNNY

> I Love you, I miss you. Indio wants to talk to you.

INDIO

> Dollar we miss you so much. We gonna get you outa there even if I gotta come break you out myself.

Six months later. In a courtroom packed with the public, and news media with cameras flashing, Dollar Bill dressed in a grey, Versace suit with matching gators, is seated at the defendants table between his attorneys, prison guards standing behind him.

JUDGE

Will the defendant please rise.

Dollar Bill stands up.

JUDGE

Shawn Watson, for the murder of Stacey Simms, we the court and the jury find you guilty of the charge of first degree murder and sentence you to life in prison. This court room is now adjourned.

The judge slams down her gavel. The prison guards handcuff Dollar Bill. As they walk him out of the court room. he looks over his shoulder at his mom, his brother, Sunny, Indio and Mya, watching him, and crying uncontrollably.

THE END